Trinity made it to the end of the corridor before Mason stopped her.

He didn't put a hand on her. Didn't tell her to stop. Didn't remind her that she was part of a criminal investigation and that she couldn't leave. She could have ignored any of those things.

"They think you're my girlfriend," he said instead. "The guys who broke into my house."

"Why would they think that?"

"I thought maybe you could answer that question."

"I can't." She started walking again. She wanted to pretend Mason's words hadn't changed things, but she couldn't. She knew that mistaken identity could get a person kidnapped or killed. Or both.

"You can't run away from your troubles, Trinity," Mason said, stepping in front of her. "Where are you planning to run?"

"Telling you that would defeat the purpose of going into hiding."

"Hiding from me isn't going to be a possibility," Mason said. "You're either part of whatever went down tonight—"

"I'm not."

"Or you've walked into something that could cause you a lot of trouble."

"I can handle it."

"You could have died tonight," he pointed out, his voice sharp-edged with irritation. "If I hadn't come home, you probably would have."

She didn't respond. There wasn't much she could say. He was right. They both knew it.

Aside from her faith and her family, there's not much **Shirlee McCoy** enjoys more than a good book! When she's not teaching or chauffeuring her five kids, she can usually be found plotting her next Love Inspired Suspense story or wandering around the beautiful Inland Northwest in search of inspiration. Shirlee loves to hear from readers. If you have time, drop her a line at shirlee@shirleemccoy.com.

Books by Shirlee McCoy

Love Inspired Suspense

Mission: Rescue

Protective Instincts
Her Christmas Guardian
Exit Strategy
Deadly Christmas Secrets
Mystery Child
The Christmas Target
Mistaken Identity

Heroes for Hire

Running for Cover
Running Scared
Running Blind
Lone Defender
Private Eye Protector
Undercover Bodyguard
Navy SEAL Rescuer
Fugitive
Defender for Hire

Visit the Author Profile page
at Harlequin.com for more titles.

MISTAKEN IDENTITY

SHIRLEE MCCOY

HARLEQUIN® LOVE INSPIRED® SUSPENSE

Recycling programs for this product may not exist in your area.

ISBN-13: 978-0-373-45692-5

Mistaken Identity

This edition published by arrangement with Love Inspired Books.

www.Harlequin.com

Printed in U.S.A.

Even in my suffering I was comforted
because your promise gave me life.
—*Psalms* 119:50

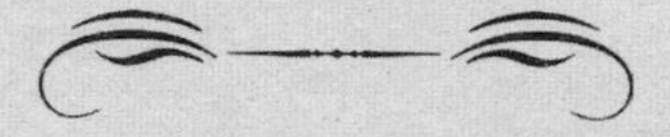

To Sharon. You know why. I love you, friend!

ONE

Trinity Miller didn't scare easily, but she was scared now.

It wasn't the darkness of the woods that stretched out to either side of the old dirt road that had her rattled. It wasn't the full moon hovering over mountain vistas. It wasn't even the silence in her old Jeep Cherokee that was getting to her.

It was the weird feeling she had.

The one that seemed to be telling her to turn around and leave. If she'd told either of her brothers about it, they'd have said she should listen. Of course, she hadn't told Jackson or Chance what she was doing. They both thought she was on a weekend jaunt to New England to see the fall foliage, eat the crisp, ripe apples. Decide what direction she wanted her life to go.

All of those things were true.

There just happened to be a couple of tiny little details that she hadn't offered. Like the fact that she was going to pay a visit to a man who was notoriously private. Like the fact that he lived in Middle-of-Nowhere, Maine.

Like the fact that she hadn't told Mason Gains she was coming or asked permission to drive down the road that had been clearly marked with no-trespassing signs.

Yeah. She'd skipped a few details when she'd been explaining things to her brothers. They'd been too busy with their work and their families to notice she was hedging around questions and offering minimal details. Twelve hours ago, when she'd left her Annapolis home and headed north, she'd been happy about that.

Now, with fear sitting like a hard rock in her belly, she wouldn't have minded having one or the other of her brothers sitting beside her.

Go home.

That's what they'd have wanted her to do. Knowing them, they'd have found a way to send her packing so they could handle the situation themselves.

Whatever the situation was.

She frowned. It wasn't like she was heading into a hostage rescue mission. She was going to talk to a guy who made prosthetic limbs for a living. How dangerous could it be?

Unless Mason Gains had a gun and decided to shoot first and ask questions later, Trinity should be just fine. She'd done her research, used her computer forensic background to find out everything she could about Mason. She hadn't found any hint of violence, any indication that he'd been in trouble with the law. He'd served his country, gone to college, gone into business doing something that could enhance the lives of wounded warriors.

He was a hero.

Heroes didn't shoot unarmed women.

She hoped.

If they did, there were sure a lot of places to hide a body around here.

At least Bryn knew where Trinity was. If she didn't return home, she could count on her best friend to let everyone know where she'd been and what she'd been up to.

By that time, it would be too late, of course.

Trinity would be buried somewhere in the forest, her body concealed under layers of dirt, dead leaves and fallen pine needles. She frowned. That was not a good direction for her thoughts to go. Not when she was already scared.

"You shouldn't be scared," she muttered, breaking the eerie silence.

Sure, she was in the middle of nowhere. Sure, there was nothing but trees and mountains as far as the eye could see, but she'd been hiking in rougher areas. She worked search and rescue, and she'd been out on rainy nights and snowy ones, serving as a flanker for K-9 teams. She'd trekked through mountains and wetland, and she'd done it without even a shiver of alarm, so she had no reason to be sitting in her locked Jeep, her heart pounding with fear as she drove down a pitch-black mountain road.

She leaned forward to ease the tension from her lower back. She'd been driving for hours, just stopping long enough to gas up and move on. Mason Gains didn't like being interrupted. He had important work to do, and he couldn't be bothered with unexpected visitors. He'd made that clear in a couple of interviews he'd done. Both had been taped several years ago. Since then he'd been quiet, living and working—according to his company website—somewhere in New England.

It had taken just under two weeks for Trinity to figure out exactly where that was. For the first time in longer than she cared to remember, she felt like her expertise in computer forensics was paying off in a way that would really matter to someone she cared about.

In ten days Bryn's son Henry would have surgery to remove his left leg. The cancer that was growing in his bone could almost certainly be stopped that way. So could his running dreams. An all-star athlete, he'd been training for Junior Olympics and Bryn had been told that he'd go even farther than that. Henry had his Navy SEAL father's drive, but he didn't have his father. Rick had been killed in Iraq when Henry was a toddler. Bryn had been working her butt off ever since, trying to be mother and father to their son.

This newest blow had shaken her, and Trinity was doing everything she could to buoy her.

This journey was part of that.

It was possible Mason would turn her away at the door. It was possible he'd refuse to hear her out. It was even more possible that he'd listen and then tell her what she already knew—he only made prosthetic limbs for veterans. He didn't work with kids.

She'd still had to come. She'd had to try.

She'd just rather not die doing it.

She eyed the dark trees, the distant mountains and the road that stretched out in front of her. Not a light. Not a house. Not any sign of civilization. Maybe she should turn around; return when the sun came up.

"Five minutes," she whispered because the silence was starting to get to her and the only thing she was getting on her radio was static. "If I don't see something by then, I'm turning around."

The wind howled, sweeping through the forest and swirling along the road. Normally, Trinity loved storms, but if one was blowing in, she didn't want to be on a dirt road in an area with spotty reception. Even Jeeps could get stuck in mud or crushed by falling trees.

So, that was that.

She was turning around.

She'd drive the fifty miles to Whisper Lake and find the little bed-and-breakfast she'd reserved a room in. She'd get a good night's sleep and she'd come at the problem fresh in the morning. Obviously she'd miscalculated the distance to Mason's property. For all she knew, she wasn't even on the right road. Aside from the no-trespassing signs, the road wasn't marked. She had no idea what the street address for the house was. She didn't even know if there was one. All she knew was what she'd found by accessing public records—Mason Gains owned two-thousand acres of land somewhere very close to where she was driving.

She slowed, trying to find a wide enough spot to turn around, and caught something in her periphery. A light glimmered through the trees to her left.

A window? It looked like it, and if there was a window, there had to be a house.

Her pulse jumped and she accelerated again, following the curve of the road through the trees and out into the open. The road ended there, stopping abruptly at the edge of a grassy field.

A mile out, a house jutted up against the blue-black sky, the forest pushing in behind it, crowding close enough that Trinity couldn't see where the house ended and the forest began.

That had to be Mason's house.

At least, she hoped it was his house.

If it wasn't, she was about to walk across a field and knock on a stranger's door.

Who was she kidding?

Mason was a stranger.

He wasn't going to be happy to see her. She was going, anyway. She'd promised Bryn that she'd try, and that meant giving her best effort.

Hopefully it wouldn't get her killed.

She shoved her phone and keys in her jacket pocket and got out of the Jeep. The early fall air already held a hint of bitter winter, the moisture in it biting and cold. Lights spilled out of several windows of the ranch-style house. She could see the details more clearly as she approached—the wrap-around porch, whitewashed and gleaming. The black door and gray siding. No shrubs or bushes butted up against the house. No trees. No fences. Nothing that would impede the owner's view of the road and the field.

That didn't make Trinity feel any more comfortable with the situation. Mason had served three tours overseas. He'd been a helicopter pilot and had seen his share of combat. It was possible that—like so many of the men and women he worked with—he had PTSD. If he did, he might be even less likely to appreciate a random stranger showing up at nine in the evening.

She walked up the porch steps, pulling her cell phone out of her pocket as she went. She didn't know if she had cell reception, but she felt better holding on to the possibility.

She knocked, the sound echoing through the night. A bird startled from a tree, a critter scurried under the porch, but no one came to the door.

She knocked again, thought she saw one of the curtains in the front window move. Someone was there. She could feel him watching as she stepped back off the porch.

"Mason?" she called, surprised at the tremor she heard in her voice.

Nerves weren't her style any more than fear was.

No response. Just the same silent house and that little flutter of curtain movement.

Someone was definitely in there.

Since he hadn't shouted for her to leave or pointed a gun in her direction, she was going to keep trying to get him to open the door. Bryn was waiting for the mission-accomplished call and Trinity planned to make it. Mason Gains was the best at what he did. His prosthetic devices were used by some of the highest level athletes in the world. Getting him to agree to make one for Henry would lift the tween's spirits and give him back the hope he'd lost the day he'd been told he was going to lose his leg. That was what Bryn wanted more than anything, and it was what Trinity wanted for her.

She walked around the side of the house. The windows were dark there, the moon the only light. The backyard was a tiny stretch of grass that bumped about against deep woods. To the right, a section had been cleared for a large workshop and a three-stall garage. An SUV sat in front of one stall, its windows tinted.

Washington, DC, license plate.

Mason must have visitors.

Good. He'd be less likely to shoot her and dump her body if there were witnesses around.

"Not funny, Trin," she muttered as she walked up the three stairs that led to a small deck.

She planned to knock on the back door, but it was open, a screen the only thing separating her from the room beyond. A kitchen, maybe. She thought she could see the outline of a refrigerator in the darkness, see what looked like a table and chairs, and something else. A person? It looked like it. Not moving, just hanging back a few feet from the screen, watching her the way she was watching him.

She didn't call out again, didn't move closer.

Something was off. She could feel it in the frigid air and in the frantic pounding of her heart.

She stepped back, quietly, cautiously, eyes glued to person behind the screen.

The stairs were right behind her and she felt for them with her foot, afraid to turn away. Afraid that if she did, whoever was on the other side of the screen would attack.

She found the first step and moved down, her hair suddenly standing on end, her nerves alive with warning. The person didn't move. Not an inch, but the air vibrated with energy.

Everything inside told her to run and, this time, she was going with her gut.

She swung around just as a quiet click broke the silence.

She knew the sound as well as she knew the sound of her mother's voice. A gun safety being released.

She had seconds, and she used them, her feet moving almost before the sound registered. She leaped to the left, landing hard on thick grass. She stumbled, kept going, racing toward the trees as the first shot rang out.

The bullet whizzed past, slammed into a tree a few feet away, the trunk splintering, bits of it flying into Trinity's face as she ducked and kept running.

The woods were there, and she dove into thick foliage, the sound of footsteps following her. A man called out, another answered, and she knew she was in bigger trouble than she ever could have imagined.

She'd ignored all the internal warnings, all the little shivers of doubt and fear, and she'd walked in on something she shouldn't have.

Like an idiot.

Like a kid who didn't know what she was doing or how to take care of herself.

Someone snagged the back of her jacket and she fell back, her phone flying from her grasp as she fought to free herself.

Elbow to a soft stomach, fist to a nose. She palmed the guy in the chin and finally broke free of his grasp. No plan except to escape. No destination but the forest with its thick trees and dark shadows. She had no idea where she was going or what she'd do once she got there. She just knew she had to keep moving.

She raced through heavy brambles, thorns catching on her skin and clothes, tearing at her hair. Blood seeped from a long scratch on her cheek, but she didn't take time to wipe it away. She could still hear branches breaking, feet pounding, someone closing in.

Please, God. Please get me out of this, and I will always tell the entire truth instead of keeping little pieces of it to myself. I promise. Just help me, she prayed, bargaining in a way she hadn't since she was old enough to understand how useless and silly it was.

God didn't bargain.

He didn't only come around when someone was in trouble, either.

He worked in His way and in His time, and Trinity was cool with that.

She wasn't cool with dying.

She knew her eternal destiny, but she'd rather not have her body buried in the woods in Maine, her family spending the rest of their lives wondering what had happened to her the way they had always wondered what had happened to her older sister.

Behind her, someone called out, the voice deep and masculine. There was an answer from somewhere to her left, and she knew they were trying to pen her in, come at her from two sides. Or maybe even three.

She ran down a steep slope, nearly tumbling into a creek that burbled over rocks and old logs. She jumped over a narrow section, her feet sinking into mud on the far bank. She didn't stop to smooth the prints away. She could hear her pursuer charging through the woods. Closing in. And she had no way of calling for help, no one flanking her, making sure she survived.

She was alone.

The way she'd wanted it, because she'd been tired of standing in the shadows of her brothers.

Now she wished they were here.

She wished she'd been more honest about her reasons for traveling to Maine and told them exactly where she planned to be. She wished a lot of things, but wishes were about as useful as umbrellas in hurricanes.

She sprinted uphill and found herself on a narrow path that skirted a ledge. A hundred feet below, dark water shimmered in the moonlight. A lake! And, beyond that, house lights. She wasn't sure how far. A couple of miles away maybe. If she could make it there, she could knock on a door, find a phone, call for help.

If she could make it.

Someone barreled onto the path a few hundred feet to her left. She didn't think, didn't hesitate. She lowered herself over the ledge, grabbing tree branches to stop her momentum as she scrambled down. If she'd had all the time in the world, she could have made it, but time wasn't on her side, and she was rushing, moving from one handhold to the other, not checking to see if they would hold her weight. She felt one give. The earth was moist from recent rain, the roots probably barely clinging to the side of the steep hill.

She kept moving, listening to the sudden silence. The thickness of it pulsed in the air, as alive and real as her terror. Had the guy pulled his gun? Did he have night-vision goggles? Was he aiming his gun at her?

She grabbed a pine sapling, her feet slipping in her haste to escape. The sapling gave, pulling away from the ground and tumbling toward the lake, Trinity tumbling with it.

And, she knew it was over.

If the fall didn't kill her, the gunman would, and then she'd be another statistic, another tragedy, another sorrow for her family to bear.

Going to an old friend's funeral hadn't been fun.

Attending his own?

Not something Mason Gains intended to do.

He moved silently through the forest, following the trail of broken branches that led away from his house and workshop. Two-thousand acres of Maine wilderness usually kept people away. That was how he liked it.

Tonight, someone had infiltrated his sanctuary, trespassed on his property and fired a shot that he'd heard loud and clear as he was returning home. If he hadn't had the windows down, letting cold air sweep away the memory of blood and gunpowder and death that had chased him from Afghanistan and Iraq, followed him across continents and through years of therapy, he might not have heard the gunshot.

But he'd had the windows down, cold air cooling the sweat that beaded his brow, and he'd heard it. He'd known exactly what it was, and he'd known it didn't belong. This was private property bordered by a state park. No hunting allowed there. Even if there had been, it wasn't hunting season, and he was certain he hadn't heard a rifle. He'd heard a handgun. One quick, sharp, report and then silence.

He'd parked the truck on the side of the long driveway, partially hiding it behind a patch of thick shrubs he'd planted with just that purpose in mind. Then he'd taken off on foot, skirting the edge of the driveway, keeping to the shadows as he made his way to the house. He'd noticed the lights first. Then, the SUV parked near his workshop; the open back door, a light shining beyond it. He'd called the police, and then done a sweep of the exterior. There'd been a Jeep parked at the far edge of the field near an old logging road that no one ever used. No other vehicles. No sign of anyone wandering around close to the house. He'd gone inside. Quietly. Just like he'd been trained to do in the military.

There'd been one person inside the house, trying to push aside the built-in book shelves that served as a door to his office. It had taken about six seconds to disarm and apprehend the guy. Youngish with a beer belly and pasty skin, he'd blabbered on about not wanting to die. Funny how people were most remorseful after they'd been caught.

Or not.

He'd asked a few questions, made a few idle threats. Handguns were dangerous, and they were convincing. Mason always carried one, and the kid had spilled enough information to let Mason know that there were two other men. They were in the woods, hunting for Mason's girlfriend.

There was one problem with that.

Mason had no girlfriend.

So…three unknown people were wandering his property.

The police were on the way, but Mason didn't believe in waiting around for others to do what he could. He'd already tied up the kid and left him trussed like a Thanksgiving turkey, lying on the floor near the bookshelves.

Now he was going to find the other players in the game.

It shouldn't be hard. They'd left a noticeable trail, and he was having no trouble at all following it. He eased through thick undergrowth, moving along the edge of the creek that cut through his property. There were footprints in the bank. Large boots and smaller sneakers. The woman who was supposed to be his girlfriend?

She'd headed up the embankment. He followed.

The steep rise led to a ledge that looked out over Whisper Lake. Beyond that, she'd have seen the lights of Whisper—the closest town. Just a pinprick on the map. Fifteen hundred residents on a good day, and exactly the kind of place Mason would have lived if he'd wanted to live close to civilization.

He shopped in the little grocery store there.

When friends came to visit, he took them to the tackle shop, the diner, the ice cream place. There wasn't much in Whisper, but it was plenty to keep the residents happy.

A pretty little place, but it was nearly fifty miles away. No way could anyone reach it on foot from his property, but he doubted his unwanted visitor knew that. If she'd been running from someone, she probably hadn't even cared.

He could hear sirens in the distance. Other than that, the woods were silent and still, eerie in their quiet. He'd bought the property for its solitude and for its view of the lake. He'd spent plenty of time sitting in the darkness, looking out over the water, praying for answers to questions he wasn't even sure he could give voice to.

He hadn't found any, but he still enjoyed the view.

He didn't enjoy having people interrupt his work.

He had three prosthetic limbs to design and create. His team would be there Monday morning. Just like always. Mason had planned to return Sunday night but John's funeral had been a sad event with a handful of mourners, no church service, no celebration of life. Just the graveside service and John's wife, Sally, crying quietly. She'd wanted Mason to stay for a couple of days. She'd offered him a room in the single-wide trailer she and John had shared. She'd actually begged Mason to stay, but their Nyack, New York, home had seemed claustrophobic.

Or, maybe, it had been the memories that had penned him in.

It didn't matter.

He'd returned two days early and someone was on his property.

Someone who'd been able to disarm the state-of-the-art security system. Someone who'd known there was an office behind the bookshelves.

That narrowed the list to maybe three or four people who worked for him, a close friend who happened to be the town sheriff and John.

He'd betrayed Mason once. It was more than possible that he'd done it again before he'd died.

Mason skirted the ledge that looked out over the lake, eyeing the foliage below, the dark water beyond it.

A small sneaker print was pressed into the path. He used that as his guide, easing himself over the ledge and finding his footing against the rock and damp earth.

He could see evidence of hands grasping branches—snapped twigs, scuff marks in the earth. Toes pressed deep into dirt.

She'd made it about halfway down when she'd fallen. He could see the uprooted sapling, the slide of her body in pine needles. He stopped, listening to the wind rustling in the leaves, the soft lap of water against the shore below him, the sounds of the sirens drawing closer. No branches breaking. No footsteps. He felt alone. Just like he should be.

He took out his light, aiming the beam down the steep slope. He could see the direction her body had taken, the dirt and rocks that had tumbled with her.

Near the bottom, the light fell on pale skin, light brown hair. Jeans. Jacket. A woman for sure. Motionless.

Dead?

He hoped not. She might be a trespasser, but she didn't deserve to die for that. He tucked the light back in his pocket and the woman jumped up.

"Hey!" he called. "Hold on!"

She'd heard. He was certain of that.

She didn't listen.

She ran toward the lake, moving quickly enough that he wasn't all that concerned about her being injured.

He scrambled down the rest of the slope, racing across pebbly earth. She was yards ahead of him, illuminated by moonlight as she waded into the water and dove below its surface.

If he didn't get her out, she'd die there, the cold stealing her strength and her life before she even knew it was happening.

He moved along the shore, his light dancing across the dark lake. She'd gone down, and she hadn't come back up, but he could see the small ripples on the surface of the water, subtle signs that she was moving beneath it. He shrugged out of his coat, his handgun zipped into an interior pocket, unbuttoned the dress shirt he'd worn to John's funeral and dropped that on top of it.

He waited until she surfaced, her head popping up as she gulped for air.

That was it. All the opportunity he needed.

He waded into the frigid water and went after her.

TWO

The water was freezing.

That wasn't something Trinity had been thinking about when she'd decided she could swim to the lights that glimmered on the far shore. Houses. Businesses. People. She was thinking about the water temperature now. She was also thinking about how far the opposite shore really was. Farther than it looked. She was a good swimmer, but the cold was already affecting her muscles, and her movements were sluggish and slow.

She could turn back, but he was there—the man who'd been standing on the slope, shining his light down at her.

She didn't know who he was.

She didn't want to know.

She just wanted to escape him, find some place to hunker down and think through her options. She'd have to swim parallel to the shore and find a safe place to exit the lake. Preferably before hypothermia set in. At the rate things were going, that wouldn't be long. She was already shivering, her teeth chattering.

Make a plan. Stick to the plan.

That was one of Chance's mottos.

The problem was that he'd never explained what to do

if the plan wasn't working out. Probably because his plans always worked out.

Trinity's? Not so much.

Look at her relationship with Dale. She'd had it all planned out. The two years of dating. The year-long engagement. The happily-ever-after.

Only, two years had turned into three and there'd been no sign of dating ever becoming anything more. That had made her worry that maybe Dale wasn't as committed to forever as she was.

Turned out, he wasn't.

It also turned out that she would have realized that long before the three-year mark if she hadn't been so committed to her poorly conceived plan.

This plan? The one that had her swimming across the lake to safety? It was just as bad.

She glanced back at the shore. She was a few hundred yards from it. No sign of the guy who'd been chasing her. He'd probably realized she was going to die without any help from him. Maybe he was sitting in the shadows of the trees, waiting for her to drown and make his job easier.

She gritted her teeth to keep them from knocking together. There had to be a place that was safer than the beach, an area of thick foliage and deep shadows, but her eyes didn't seem to be working well and her arms didn't seem to want to paddle. Her legs felt heavy and she wanted to close her eyes and float for just long enough to regain her strength.

If she did, she'd die.

She was still coherent enough to realize that, but it wouldn't be long and her brain would slow as much as her body had. She turned toward the beach, desperate to get out of the water before that happened. All thoughts of the man and the danger he represented were gone. She had more immediate things to worry about. Like freezing to death or drowning or—

An arm wrapped around her, and she was yanked back against a hard body, her arms pinned at her sides. She tried to scream, but all that emerged was a quiet squeak. Tried to fight, but she was trapped by a steel-like arm and her own weakness.

She kicked backward, trying to free herself.

"Stop," a man growled.

But she kicked again, the icy water splashing up into her face.

"You want us both to drown?" he asked, dragging her closer to his body. They were heading toward the shore. She could feel that, and she knew the exact moment his feet touched the lake bottom, because he hefted her up like a sack of potatoes, tossing her over his shoulder in a fireman carry that forced every bit of air from her lungs.

She should have kept fighting, but the wind was howling, and she was freezing, her body trembling so violently, she thought she might shake into pieces.

Seconds later she was lowered to her feet. Gently. Surprising since she figured the guy was about to kill her.

"That was one of the stupidest things I've ever seen anyone do," he said.

"Not as stupid as firing a gun at an innocent person," she retorted.

"Equally stupid acts, lady. One will get you killed. The other could kill someone else," he growled, grabbing a coat from the ground and pulling a handgun from somewhere inside it.

Her blood went as cold as her body was, and she took a step back.

"Relax," he muttered. "If I'd wanted to hurt you, it

would have been done already. It's not like you're in any shape to fight."

"I could fight if I needed to." Maybe.

"Hopefully, you won't have to put that to the test." He checked the safety on the gun, tucked it into the waistband of his pants and tossed the coat around her shoulders.

It was still warm from his body, and she wanted to pull it over her soaked hair and huddle under it until some of the warmth seeped into her. She was afraid if she did, she'd close her eyes and wake up locked in a basement somewhere.

Or, worse, not wake up at all.

"Maybe you should think about that next time you decide to fire a shot and then chase a person through the woods. Not many people are going to take kindly to that, and most of them are going to do exactly what I did and—"

"I wasn't the one who fired the gun, and I wasn't chasing you anywhere." He lifted what looked like a white dress shirt, shook it out and pulled it on.

Unlike her, he'd been thinking before he'd dived into the lake.

His pants were soaked, but his shirt wasn't.

She, on the other hand, was still shaking with cold, her wet clothes clinging to her skin. "Look, it's freezing. How about we just call it a night? You go your way. I go mine. No harm, no foul."

"That," he murmured, "is a matter of opinion."

"What's that supposed to...?" Her voice trailed off because the moonlight was falling straight onto his face, and she knew him. Knew of him, anyway. Mason Gains. The guy she'd traveled six-hundred miles to see.

"To mean?" he finished her question as he tugged the coat closed and buttoned the top three buttons, his knuckles brushing her chin and her jaw as he turned the collar up around her ears. "It means that you're trespassing, and I've called the police. They'll be very interested in hearing your story."

"My story is simple. I came to find you, and you chased me through the woods with a gun."

"I already told you, it wasn't me."

"*Someone* chased me. I fell." And she'd hit her head. The cold had stolen most of the pain, but she could feel it again, pulsing just above her right ear. She touched the area, felt warm blood.

"You're bleeding," he commented, and she wanted to say something sarcastic, because she was cold, she was scared and she was in pain.

She didn't think that would win her any points, so she kept her mouth shut.

He sighed. "Come on. Let's go back. The police should be at the house by now."

"Good. Maybe they can find the guys who were shooting at me."

"How many?" he asked, taking her arm and leading her along the shore. They weren't heading the way they'd come. That was probably for the best. She didn't think she could climb up what she hadn't been able to climb down.

"At least two."

"Did you see them?"

"No. I was too busy running for my life to stop and get a description of the people who were trying to kill me."

Oops.

There she went with the sarcasm.

"Glad you've kept your sense of humor," Mason muttered, stepping between towering pine trees, his grip on her arm firm.

She knew he was trying to keep her from running. She couldn't say she blamed him, but she didn't like it.

"No need to hold on to me," she said, pulling her arm from his grasp. "I've got no idea where we are and no idea how to get to civilization from here. In other words, I have absolutely nowhere to go, so I'm not going anywhere but wherever you're heading."

"Thanks for the information. Now, I'll give you some. If you run, I'll catch you," he replied. "So, how about you save us both the effort and don't do it?"

"I already told you, I'm not planning on running." Especially not now when the guy she'd been looking for was just a few inches away.

They hadn't gotten off to a good start.

She could fix that, clear things up, explain all the reasons why he should hear what she had to say and listen to her reasons for being there.

They were moving steadily uphill, heading—she presumed—back toward Mason's house. She expected him to ask more questions. She actually hoped he would. She just needed an opening, and she could explain the situation with Henry, tell Mason all about the young athlete, his cancer diagnosis and his upcoming surgery.

But Mason seemed content to stay silent.

She did the same, the sound of police sirens a constant reminder that she was running out of time. For all she knew, she'd be arrested as soon as she reached Mason's house. She'd be tossed in jail for trespassing, and she'd never get an opportunity to say what she needed to.

She couldn't let that happened.

She'd promised Bryn she'd give it her best. Walking mutely through the forest with the man who could help Henry? That wasn't it.

"I'm Trinity Miller," she said, her voice a little too loud.

Nothing.

Not even a hitch in his stride.

"I have a friend—"

"No."

"You don't even know what I was going to say."

"Don't I?" He turned abruptly, stopping short in the middle of the path. It was too dark to see his expression, but Trinity was certain he wasn't smiling. "You have a friend who needs money, or an uncle who needs help, or you know a good charity I could donate money to."

"Not even close."

"Then why are you here?"

"My friend's son has cancer. He's going to have his leg amputat—"

"No," he repeated and started walking again, his long legs eating up the ground so quickly she had to jog to keep up.

"You haven't even heard me out."

"I heard enough to say no."

"I drove six hundred miles!" she protested, her teeth chattering on the last word.

She did not want to fail at this. She didn't want to have to call Bryn to tell her that she'd blown their chance.

"I'm sorry you wasted your time." He didn't sound sorry. He sounded irritated.

"Look—" she began.

Somewhere to their right, a branch broke.

Mason grabbed her wrist, yanking her close to his side.

"What—"

"Quiet," he whispered, his lips close to her ear. "I'm going to see who that is. You stay here."

"We need to stay together," she whispered back.

"It's not up for discussion." He pulled her off the path and dragged her into thick undergrowth. "Do. Not. Move."

Three words and he was gone, slipping soundlessly away while she shivered in his coat.

* * *

Another branch snapped as Mason crept through the heavy underbrush. He followed the sound, honing in on the soft pad of feet on dead leaves.

Whoever was out there, he didn't know much about being quiet. He also didn't know much about staying hidden. Mason could see a flashlight beam bouncing along the ground a few yards away. The guy was searching, but he wasn't even close to where Mason had left the woman.

Trinity Miller.

Interesting that she'd found him.

Most people who looked didn't.

He had a house in Boston he rented out, and that was where people who were searching for him usually ended up. Somehow Trinity had ended up here. He wanted to know how. He also wanted to know why. She'd said something about a friend's son and cancer, and he'd cut her off. He didn't work with kids. There were too many memories there, but he was intrigued by the thought of someone going to such great effort to help a friend. Six hundred miles to see a stranger for a friend's sake? That was a long way to travel.

If that was really the case, if she'd really driven that far, Trinity was the kind of friend everyone wanted to have.

If her claim was true.

There'd been a lot of activity around his house lately. A few days before he'd left for John's funeral, government officials paid him a visit. They'd wanted information about one of his clients. He'd refused to give it. The military police had stopped by the next day, demanding that he release confidential information. Mason had refused again.

For all he knew, Trinity worked for the government or was part of the military, sent to do what the other two groups had not—gain access to information about Tate

Whitman. Tate had served three tours in Iraq. He'd nearly lost his life there. Two years ago, Mason had fitted his prosthetic leg. Tate was an active guy. When he wasn't teaching college counterterrorism classes, he was hiking, biking, running and lifting weights.

Unfortunately, he was also the key witness in a court-martial case that had the potential to bring down some very high-level military officials. He'd gone into witness protection six months ago. Apparently, he'd run from it soon after. Now people were looking for him, and that seemed to always lead them to Mason.

It wasn't surprising. A computer chip Mason built into every prosthesis collected real-time information about the amputee's movements and muscle strength. The information was sent wirelessly to Mason's computer system. He used it to create the best prosthetic design possible for the individual. The system had a built-in tracking system that could be used to find the prosthetic if it was stolen or misplaced. In theory, it could also be used to track the amputee who was wearing it.

It would take Mason all of five minutes to figure out where Tate was. He wasn't going to. He had client confidentially to protect. Plus, he didn't trust people. Not much, anyway. If Tate had thought he needed to hide from the organization that was supposed to be protecting him, he'd had good reason for it.

It wasn't Mason's job to find out what it was. It wasn't his job to turn him over to the military police, either. Eventually Mason might be subpoenaed. For now, he'd refused the request for information.

Yeah. No. He wasn't taking Trinity's story at face-value.

He stepped into the shadow of an old elm, the heavy branches leaning toward the ground and hiding him from whoever was approaching. He could still see the light, and he watched it as it crawled along a fallen log and passed Mason's hiding place. Finally, a man stepped into sight. Tall. Lean. No weapon that Mason could see. That didn't mean much.

The perp he'd disarmed had been stupid enough to carry his gun tucked in the pocket of his jeans. This one could be hiding a weapon anywhere.

The man passed, leaves crunching under his feet, his breath heaving. He might be lean, but he wasn't in good shape. He sounded like a steam engine huffing and puffing his way through the darkness.

A man called out and Mason's quarry flicked off his light, darting back in the direction he'd come.

Mason sprinted after him, not bothering to be quiet about it. He could hear more voices—several men and at least one woman.

"Police!" one of them called as lights flashed across a nearby tree. They were on the ledge, heading down, and Mason could have stepped back and let them make the apprehension. He was annoyed, though, and just angry enough to want the guy to be stopped sooner rather than later.

He followed the perp onto the path that led to the beach, tackling him as he tried to sprint to a small dock that jutted out into the lake.

"Who are you?" Mason growled as he patted the guy down and found an ankle holster and small pistol. "What are you doing on my property?"

He kept his knee in the center of the guy's spine and checked the safety. "Did you discharge your weapon tonight?"

The guy remained silent, and Mason added a little extra pressure to his spine.

"You're going to break my back," the man gasped, finally struggling. "Get off me. I didn't do anything wrong!"

"Did you fire your weapon?"

The man shook his head.

"That a no?"

"You figure it out," he gasped.

"I'd rather move on to another question. Where's your buddy?"

"I don't have one. I was out walking alone."

"Walking, huh?"

"It's not a crime."

"It is if you're on private property while you're doing it. You have a permit for the pistol?"

"In my car. Let me up and I'll go get it."

"How about we just wait for the police and they can do it for you?"

They were charging down the slope, crashing through underbrush and thickets.

He glanced toward them, counting half a dozen lights flashing in the darkness.

"Drop the gun! Hands in the air!" one of the officers shouted and Mason did exactly what he'd been told immediately. No way was he going to take a bullet for this guy.

The pistol landed with a soft thud and officers swarmed closer.

"Facedown on the ground! Keep your hands where we can see them!"

Mason followed orders.

The perp was doing the same, staying prone on the ground, one arm straight above his head, the other…

Moving.

Subtly.

Reaching for the gun that was a few feet away.

"Don't," Mason warned, but it was too late, the guy lunged toward the weapon, lifting it as he tried to run.

Mason dropped to the ground as the first bullet flew, the police yelling commands, the scent of gunfire in the air. The crack and pop and zing of weapons being discharged, and for a moment he was back in time, lying on the hot sand of an Iraqi outpost while bullets whizzed over his head.

THREE

Five rounds fired in quick succession.

Law enforcement officers yelled commands.

And, then, silence. To Trinity, that was the worst sound of all—the emptiness and quiet filled with the echo of violence.

She stepped from her hiding place, searching for the path that would lead her back to the beach. She was almost certain that's where the gunfire had come from. The police were there. That being the case, she should be safe enough.

She hoped, because she wasn't going to keep cowering in her hiding place. Not while Mason faced down the men who'd been chasing her through the woods. She'd caused her own trouble, and she was going to get herself out of it.

Once she did, she'd concentrate on getting what she'd come to Maine for.

That was going to prove difficult since Mason had already refused to hear her out. He was angry that she'd trespassed, irritated that she'd gotten herself embroiled in a mess on his property and probably anxious to see her leave the area.

She had a weekend to change things.

A weekend to convince him to listen.

First, she had to make sure he was okay.

The moon had inched above the trees, and it glowed gold-green, illuminating the dead leaves and scrub that littered the forest floor. The path should be right up ahead, and she headed in that direction, moving as quietly as she could, afraid to break the ominous silence.

She reached the path and hesitated, her skin crawling, her pulse racing. Voices carried through the trees, drifting up from the beach. None of them frantic or excited. Whatever had happened, whatever the gunfire had meant, it was over, but Trinity still felt uneasy.

She stepped onto the path and turned toward the beach, skirting past giant pine trees that could have been hiding anyone or anything.

Sounds drifted up from the shore, men and women talking, a dog barking, radios buzzing with activity.

She thought about calling out, but she was afraid of who else might be listening. Not just the law-enforcement officials who'd converged on the property. There'd been at least two men in the woods and it was possible both of them were still free.

She shivered, her teeth chattering as she jogged toward the beach. The slope was easy, but her feet were numb and she could barely feel the ground beneath them. She tripped over roots, stumbled over rocks. Her foot got caught in a tangle of weeds spreading across the path and she fell hard.

Someone grabbed her arm, dragged her up.

She went fighting, swinging her fist toward a shadowy face.

"Let's not," Mason growled, snagging her hand before she could make contact.

"How did you get here?" she asked, taking a couple of quick steps back to put some distance between them.

"I walked. Now, how about you tell me why you didn't stay where I left you."

"I heard gunshots."

"And that made you think you should jump into whatever chaos was happening?"

"The gunfire stopped. I heard the police. I figured it was safe enough to come out."

"Just like you figured it was safe enough to swim in a lake that has a temperature hovering in the thirties?"

"For the record," she said, "I wasn't exactly thinking when I jumped into the lake."

"For the record," he replied, cupping her elbow and tugging her along the path. "I like quiet. I like peace. I do not like people bringing drama to my property."

"I didn't bring this. It was here when I arrived."

"If you'd stayed away, you wouldn't have walked into it."

"If I'd stayed away, I wouldn't have had the opportunity to meet you. Which was the entire purpose of my trip to Maine."

"Normal people don't travel six hundred miles to meet with strangers. Especially if the strangers they plan to meet don't know they're coming."

"I never said I was normal." She pulled his coat a little closer, using the movement to dislodge his hand from her elbow.

"If you're not, then we have something in common." He grabbed her arm, and this time she didn't think she was going to maneuver away from him. "Because I'm not the typical hospitable rural resident who'd happily offer food and ride to someone who broke down in front of his house. I don't like unexpected visitors, Trinity. Generally speaking, I ignore them."

"I got that impression from the interviews you did a couple of years back."

"I don't like having my work interrupted," he continued as if she hadn't spoken. "And, I for sure don't like to be lied to, manipulated, or used."

"I hope you're not implying that I'm trying to do any of those things."

"The timing of your arrival is suspect."

"What does that mean?"

"The sheriff wants to speak with you."

"If you're trying to scare me, it's not working. I didn't do anything wrong, and I'm happy to speak with the sheriff."

"I'm sure Judah will be happy to hear that."

"Judah?"

"Dillon. He's the sheriff. We've been friends for a long time."

"Sounds like you're still trying to scare me."

"Why would I? Unless you've done something wrong, you've got nothing to be scared of."

He'd given her an opening, another opportunity to try to tell him about Henry. She wasn't going to miss it. "I already told you, I'm here for a friend. Her son has cancer in his right femur, and the leg will have to be amputated. I came to—"

"You can tell Judah. He'll be able to fact-check."

"Is there some reason why you don't want to hear what I have to say?"

"Aside from the things I already mentioned? No."

"Then maybe I should clear things up for you. I have no intention of lying to you, of using you or of manipulating you."

"I noticed you didn't mention not arriving unexpectedly, not bringing chaos and not distracting me from my work."

"I didn't bring chaos, and—"

"Tell that to the guy who's bleeding on the beach."

"Was he shot?" she asked, hurrying along beside him.

"Yes."

"Was he one of the guys who chased me through the woods?"

"I have no idea. He did have a gun."

"Is he dead?"

"Not yet."

"Is he going to die?"

"How about we play Twenty Questions after you talk to the sheriff?"

She'd rather ask the questions now, but she had the feeling she'd pushed Mason as far as he was willing to be pushed. Any more questions and he might shut her out completely. That would make it a lot more difficult to broach the subject of Henry again.

She pressed her lips together, sealing in a dozen more things she wanted to ask.

Let him have what he wanted—silence and peace.

For now.

They reached the beach and stepped off the trail, heading toward a group of people standing near the water's edge. Several more people were kneeling beside a prone figure. A man. Trinity couldn't see his face, but she could see the dark blood spreading beneath him. A lot of blood. Too much. If they didn't get him to the hospital soon, he'd die. The tense silence of the crowd said they knew it.

Someone stepped away from the group, walking toward Trinity and Mason with a long brisk stride that reminded her of her Chance. Her oldest brother had a way of commanding attention without even trying. This guy seemed to do the same. He met her eyes as he approached.

"Ma'am," he said. "I'm Sheriff Judah Dillon, Whisper Sheriff's Department."

"I'm Trinity Miller."

"From Annapolis, Maryland," he said. "We ran the

plates on your Jeep. You want to tell me what brought you to Whisper?" he asked.

"I came to see Mason."

"He says he doesn't know you."

"He doesn't. I wanted to speak with him about a friend." She glanced at Mason. He was watching her dispassionately and didn't seem inclined to verify her story.

"I see," the sheriff said.

It was obvious that he didn't. He hadn't asked enough questions to understand her motive, and it didn't look like he was going to.

"Sheriff—" she began, but he raised a hand, cutting her off.

"I'll have a deputy take you to the station. You can warm up there. I'll take your statement when I finish here."

"I'd rather not—"

Too late, he'd already motioned to a young-looking deputy who seemed eager to do whatever the sheriff wanted. What he wanted was to get Trinity out of the way.

"Get her some coffee and let her wait in my office. We'll make a decision about pressing charges after I figure out what's going on," he said as the deputy took her arm and started leading her away.

"Charges? For what?" she protested, suddenly understanding something her nearly frozen brain hadn't been able to process before. They thought she was a criminal, that she was someone connected to the guy who was lying on the ground bleeding.

"We'll make that decision later," the sheriff repeated, already turning away and walking back toward the fallen man.

"But, I haven't done anything wrong!"

"Ma'am," the sheriff said, turning to face her again.

"Trespassing is a misdemeanor offense. I don't think I need to explain that to you."

"But—"

He was moving again, and Mason was walking with him, the two of them talking quietly, probably discussing whatever trumped-up charges they planned to make.

Then again, she had trespassed. That wasn't trumped up, and she couldn't even say she wasn't guilty if the sheriff decided to book her on the charges.

"This is all a mistake," she said, but the deputy didn't respond. He had his mission, and he seemed intent on it. Maybe he wanted to prove himself. He was young. Probably a couple of years younger than her. He couldn't have been a deputy for long.

"It really is a mistake." She tried again, and this time he did look at her, his dark eyes gleaming in the moonlight.

"It'll all get sorted out. Right now, let's just concentrate on getting you inside and warmed up."

They'd reached the path, and she wanted to yank her arm from his, run back to Mason and the sheriff and explain herself.

But she thought that might cause more trouble than she already had, so she kept moving, stepping onto the path and glancing back.

Mason had stopped halfway to the crowd of people and had turned in her direction. His face was hidden in shadows, but she thought he might have been smiling.

Trinity looked like she was being led to the gallows, and she was eyeing Mason as if he were the reason for it. In point of fact, he was. He'd asked Judah to have her transported to the station. He hadn't wanted to expend energy keeping an eye on her, and he was still uncertain of her status. She was either a criminal or an innocent bystander.

Until he knew for sure which she was, he wasn't giving her the opportunity to escape.

"You know I can't hold her there for long, right?" Judah asked as Trinity and the deputy stepped onto the path and disappeared from view.

"You don't need to hold her for any longer than it takes to get her statement. I just need her out of the way. I don't want to deal with more chaos than I've already got."

"You don't have chaos. I do. It's my town, my jurisdiction. My problem. I'll take care of it. All you need to do is answer questions and stay out of the way."

"You know that's not going happen, right?"

"Yeah, but I thought I'd give it a shot. You really think Trinity has something to do with this?" He waved toward the fallen man. EMTs were lifting him onto a stretcher, and Mason thought he could smell the scent of blood in the chilly night air. His stomach heaved, but he ignored it.

"I'm not sure, but I'm not much into coincidence," he responded and was relieved that his tone was even and controlled. He'd spent years learning to compartmentalize the past, keep it tucked neatly away so that he could be in traumatic situations and not panic.

"Me, neither. Which is why it strikes me as odd that your house was broken into on a night when you were supposed to be out of town. Who knew you were going to the funeral?"

"You and John's widow, Sally. That about covers it."

"And, Sally knew you were coming back tonight? I was under the impression you'd be away until Sunday."

"That was the plan. It changed."

"Because?"

"I attended the funeral out of a sense of obligation, but John and I weren't exactly buddies these last few years, and I've never been all that fond of his wife. I thought she might need help settling John's estate, but all she really wanted to do was sob in my arms. I decided to cut the trip short."

"Was she happy about that?"

"She tried to convince me to stay. At least for another night. So that she didn't have to face the empty house." Those had been her exact words. When he'd refused to stay the night, she'd begged him to stay for a couple more hours. Through dinner. Or lunch.

"She knows what happened between you and John, right?"

"They were married when he and I were business partners. Seeing as how he signed over his share of our company in exchange for me not pressing charges, I'd say she does."

"You should have pressed charges," Judah said.

Maybe, but Mason had partially blamed himself for what had happened. He hadn't wanted to deal with the financial aspects of the company. He'd left it to John, trusting him because they'd been army buddies and friends. He'd known John's weakness—that he drank too much, partied too hard, sometimes hung with the wrong kind of people. He'd also known that John was a computer programming whiz. It was his program that allowed Mason to design the kind of prosthetics he created. John was also the one who'd had the idea of implanting a computer chip into the prosthetic limb. If he'd been honest, if he'd played by the rules, if he hadn't cheated someone he'd called friend, he'd have died a millionaire. Instead, he and Sally had been living in a single-wide trailer in a run-down trailer park.

Mason tried not to think about that, tried not to wonder if he should have handled things differently when he'd found out about John's crimes.

"Instead of pressing charges, I got his half of the company," he said.

That had been the agreement.

The quarter of a million dollars John had syphoned from their business account had been a little more than half the value of the company. In exchange for not having charges brought against him and not having to repay the money, John had agreed to hand the company over to Mason.

"In my opinion, you let him off easy, but we've talked it out a dozen times. The past is past. What I'm wondering now is what tonight has to do with John and his widow."

"Maybe nothing."

"You really think that?" Judah eyed the EMTs who were carrying the injured man away.

"No. John and I were still working together when I had this house built. He knew I had a hidden office, and he knew I was keeping sensitive material there."

"And you think he sent someone here to access that material?"

"Have you heard of Tate Whitman?"

"The name is vaguely familiar."

"You know that court-martial case that's been all over the news?"

"Bigwig army general accused of selling information that got half his battalion killed? Who doesn't know about it?"

"Tate is the star witness in the case. He's also one of my clients. He entered witness protection a while back. Last week, a couple of government officials came here asking for information about his whereabouts. The MPs came, too. Apparently he's on the run."

"And they think you can find him?"

"I can find him. I won't. There are tracking devices in all my prosthetics, Judah. They're part of the program that allows me to design the best possible limb for the client.

It's common knowledge among people who work with me. I'm contracted by several government agencies, so there's no secret to what I do and how I do it. They want to track Tate using that chip. I refused to allow it."

"Do you think the guys who came tonight are feds?"

"No. Their work was too sloppy."

"Then what *do* you think?"

"If the MPs and the feds are looking for information about Tate here, they probably aren't the only ones. If Tate doesn't testify, it's going to make the case against the general really hard to prove."

"You think someone affiliated with the general knows you have the ability to track Tate?"

"It makes as much sense as anything else does."

"If that's true, the information could have come from one of your employees or from—"

"John? Exactly. He was my first thought. For the right price, he'd sell his own mother out." He sounded bitter, and he didn't like it. He'd forgiven John a long time ago. He didn't trust him. He wasn't friends with him. But he had forgiven.

"What about his wife? Would she do the same?"

"Sally? She's an unknown to me. We were never friends, and I'm not sure what she's capable of."

"I'll check her out. See what I can dig up. If she and John were passing information along, we can probably assume they were getting paid for it. I'll get a warrant to access bank and cell phone records. It could take a few days, but I think I can prove probable cause."

"I don't know how much John shared with her. He might have told her everything about the way the prosthetics are designed, or he might have told her nothing. They had a rocky relationship most of the—"

A gunshot rang out, cutting off Mason's words.

Seconds later a woman screamed, the sound chilling Mason's blood.

Trinity.

It had to be.

He took off, sprinting toward the trees. He didn't know the woman, he wasn't sure of her agenda, but he didn't want her hurt. He sure didn't want her killed.

She'd made her way onto his property.

He needed to make certain she made it off. Alive. Unharmed. Capable of answering all the questions he needed to ask.

FOUR

"Don't scream again. You hear me?"

Trinity heard. Loud and clear.

She was going to listen, because the guy had the barrel of his gun pressed to her jaw. She could feel the metal digging into her skin, but it didn't hurt. Maybe it did, and she was just too scared to feel it.

"I said," he growled, slamming the gun into her face, "did you hear me?"

"Yes," she bit out, and he shoved her forward with his body, one arm around her waist, the other around her shoulder, that gun still pressed against her jaw. They were moving fast, and she was terrified of tripping and causing him to pull the trigger. She doubted he'd care if that happened.

He'd shot an officer of the law. He wasn't planning to be caught. She wasn't planning to be kidnapped. She needed to get back to the deputy. He'd been shot in the chest, but she hadn't seen any blood. If he'd been wearing a Kevlar vest under his shirt, he should be okay, but she'd barely had time to feel for a pulse before she'd been dragged into the forest.

One scream. That's all she'd had time for.

It didn't matter. Between the gunshot and her scream,

there was no way the sheriff hadn't been alerted to the trouble. Help would arrive. Eventually. She just hoped eventually wasn't sometime after the guy got her to his vehicle. She knew how these things worked. Once she was in a car traveling away from the scene, her chances of survival went from grim to none.

They moved through dense forest, branches and twigs snagging in Trinity's hair and pulling at her still-wet clothes. She couldn't feel the cold any more than she'd felt pain. Adrenaline was a gift God gave people to get them out of terrible situations. She hoped it would be enough to get her out of this one. Her family would be devastated if something happened to her. Her brothers would probably blame themselves. Her parents would, too.

She'd be safe in the arms of Jesus—just like the old song said—and they'd be left to move on without her. Only they wouldn't be able to move on any more than they'd been able to move on after her sister had been kidnapped. They'd spend every holiday leaving a place at the table for her. They'd visit her grave and put flowers there. They'd wonder what they could have done to help her, and she wouldn't be there to remind them that she'd made her own stupid choices and gotten her own not-so-great consequences.

Just thinking about it made her tear up. Of course, she'd thought this through before she'd decided to come, but in all her thinking, she'd never imagined getting into a situation where she might actually die.

The forest opened onto an old logging road, the dirt deeply rutted from years of heavy trucks hauling out logs. Even now, decades after the last load had been transported, the ruts were still there, deep, black lines in the packed earth. She stumbled into one, her ankle twisting, pain shooting up her leg. She went down hard, the guy's hold loosening as he lost his balance, the gun falling away. No explosion of bullets. No violent report.

She didn't think. She didn't need to. She'd practiced the move hundreds of times with her brothers. She grabbed the guy's forearm, yanking him toward her with enough force to send him flying. She was on her feet before he landed, darting into the trees, searching for shadowy areas to hide in. There were plenty of them. There were also twigs, branches, thorns, roots. She tripped and flew into a tree, bouncing off and landing with a loud crash that carried through the darkness.

She thought she could hear the guy coming after her, running through the forest in pursuit. She didn't know who he was. She didn't know what he wanted. She wasn't going to wait around to find out. She also wasn't going to try to outrun him. She was making too much noise and she'd be too easy to track.

She eased between trees, forcing herself to slow down, to be quiet, to urge a little calm into her frantic heartbeat. She could do this. She had to do this. Think. Act. Escape.

Except she wasn't sure where she'd be escaping to.

The woods were dense, the foliage tangled masses of thorny brambles. She could get lost out here. She could lose her bearings and wander so far away no one would ever find her. Safe from the gunman and undone by her own terrible sense of direction.

She stopped, listened.

He was behind her, pushing through the thick patch of brambles she'd just run through. In the distance, men and women were calling out to one another. A dog barked and sirens screamed. Lots of help, but all of it too far away to do her any good.

She had to switch gears. Be smart rather than fast.

She moved silently, ducking under the heavy bough of

a pine tree and grabbing hold of one of the lower branches. This would be an easy climb and a better option than fleeing. She scrambled up, perching on a thick branch and waiting as her pursuer thundered past. Rain dripped through the umbrella of pine needles, landing on her head and her exposed neck. She still had Mason's coat, but her clothes clung to her nearly frozen skin and she shivered, the tremors shaking the branch and sending pine needles tumbling.

If he returned, he'd notice.

If he noticed, she'd be trapped. Nowhere to go but down, straight into his waiting arms. She could still hear people in the distance. She thought about shouting for help but the gunman might return before help arrived.

She waited another few heartbeats, listening as the voices drew closer. Nature was its own kind of song and she was hearing it in the drip of rain and patter of ice, her heartbeat the backdrop rhythm to which it all played.

She felt lulled by it and by the cold that had seeped through to her bones. If she waited any longer, she'd fall asleep in the crook of the old pine tree, her body slowly freezing as the temperature dropped.

Not a good image and not any more pleasant to think about than being kidnapped.

Her movements were sluggish as she climbed down, her efforts clumsy. Her fingers felt thick and stiff, her grip tenuous. She should have thought this trip through a little more. She should have consulted with her brothers. They would have insisted on coming along, and she'd have let them, because she loved them and hated to upset her family.

Should have. Could have.

Hadn't.

Now she was alone—just like she'd wanted to be. She'd

have to figure things out on her own. Just like she'd planned. She'd have to face things head-on. She'd have to do what she'd been telling her brothers she could for years.

Her feet slipped and she fell, her hands grasping a branch as she tumbled. She jerked to a stop, body dangling for a split second before she realized she was right above the forest floor. A quick drop and she was down. Breathless. Cold. Alive.

She just had to stay that way.

She wanted to walk back the way she'd come, but every direction looked the same. She'd spent childhood summers camping with her parents and brothers. She'd hiked parts of the Appalachian Trail with friends. She was used to rough terrain and thick forest, but she wasn't use to navigating without a compass.

"You should have thought of that before you came here," she muttered.

"Thought of what?" someone asked, and she jumped, whirling around to face the shadowy figure of a man.

She didn't panic. She was too cold for that. She didn't run, because her slow-moving brain finally recognized the voice.

"Mason," she said. "I thought you were down near the lake."

"I'm not," he said. "I heard the gunshot. Where did he go?"

"There's a logging road somewhere through there." She pointed in what she hoped was the direction of the road.

"I know it. It's actually to the west," he corrected, gesturing in the opposite direction.

"He brought me there, so I think he might have a ride waiting."

"That's not what I wanted to hear," he said, pulling out his cell phone and sending a quick text. "Judah will send some cars out, but the guy is probably long gone by now. *If* he's smart. That's up for debate."

"He was smart enough to figure out how to get into your house," she pointed out.

"I didn't make it difficult to get in. Not for someone who's trained to do it," he said, not offering any details or giving any reasons.

"You don't have a security system?"

"Yes. I also have cameras. Unless he wore a mask, he's on the security footage."

"The FBI has face-match technology. They can probably figure out who he was."

"How about you let law enforcement worry about that. You have enough problems of your own," he responded. "You're in trouble. Probably more than you imagined when you came out here tonight."

"That's an understatement."

"So maybe it's time to rethink things and take a new approach to the situation."

"I drove out to see you. I can't undo that." She started walking, and he grabbed her elbow, forced her into a one-eighty.

"My place is the other way," he murmured. "And I'm not talking about undoing anything. I'm talking about coming clean."

"About?"

"Your reason for being out here tonight."

"I already told you my reason." But she'd be happy to tell him again, because the more she told him about Henry, the easier it might be to convince him to help. "My friend's son has cancer. He's an athlete. A runner. Probably Olympic-level one day," she continued in a rush, hoping to get the whole story out before he cut her off. "He's going to lose his leg, and I promised his mother that I'd—"

"You know how easy it will be to check your story, right?" he cut in.

"I'll be happy to give you Bryn's number."

"She's the friend?"

"She's more than a friend. We're like sisters. I've known her for most of my life."

"So she'd lie for you?"

"That would depend on the circumstances."

"Let's say the circumstances were you going to jail. Or not." He pushed through thick brambles, holding a branch as she followed.

"That would depend on my guilt or innocence. If I were innocent and she knew it, she might lie to help me," she admitted.

"I see."

"No. You don't. If I were going to make up a story to get myself out of trouble, it wouldn't be one that involved my best friend. First, because I wouldn't want to pull her into my trouble, and second, because I'd figure that you wouldn't believe a word she said."

"You'd be right about that," he responded.

"You want a little more truth? I make my living getting people in and out of really tough situations. I know how to spin a story and how to plant plenty of evidence to make that story seem true." It's what she did at her brothers' company. HEART was a hostage rescue team, a cohesive unit of men and women who reunited families and rescued people from terrible situations. Trinity was glorified office help. She did the research before missions, created travel plans and coordinated the missions from home. When there was trouble, she often contacted local authorities in places like South Africa, China, Egypt. Sometimes, she had to get team members out of really dicey situations. When that happened, she said what needed to be said to save their lives.

"I'm surprised you're admitting that," Mason said.

"I'm admitting it because I don't have anything to hide. I came out here to try to help a friend. I'm hoping I'll still be able to do that."

He didn't respond.

She wanted to try to get some kind of reaction out of him, but her teeth were chattering and she was shaking so hard she could barely walk. She wanted out of the woods. She wanted a nice warm room, to be wrapped in a nice warm blanket, far away from the icy rain and the guy with the gun.

Maybe adventure wasn't her thing, after all.

She'd thought it was when she'd been sitting at the desk in her office in DC, pouring through internet files and old documents. But maybe the idea of going on rescue missions with her brothers had been as silly and childish as they'd always seemed to think. Maybe she really *wasn't* cut out for this kind of thing, and maybe she'd be smart to acknowledge it. At least to herself.

Then again, maybe she was just frozen and tired, her thinking clouded by cold and fatigue. Maybe she'd done just fine escaping the gunman, coming up with a plan to keep from being kidnapped, proving to herself that all the hours of in-class, self-defense training had paid off.

She tripped and Mason's hand shifted from her elbow to her waist. She couldn't feel it. Not through the layers of cloth and ice.

"I'm okay," she said as if he'd asked.

"Our ideas of what okay means are vastly different," he responded.

"I'm alive. I'm moving. I'm..." She couldn't think of any other positives.

"Freezing?" he supplied.

"I'm too cold to know for sure, but it's a good possibility."

She thought he chuckled but she might have been mistaken. Her ears were as cold as the rest of her.

"They'll warm you up when you get to the police station. Hot coffee. Blankets." He steered her through the woods without any hesitation. Obviously he didn't need a compass, a guide, a helping hand.

"I'd rather go to the hospital," she responded.

"You're hurt?"

"I'm worried about the deputy who was shot." That was true. She *was* worried, but she also thought she'd have a better chance of walking out of a hospital than she would the sheriff's department. Aside from trespassing, she hadn't done anything wrong. She knew that but she wasn't sure the sheriff did, and she was certain Mason didn't. She needed to find a place to go to ground, contact her brothers and get some help. Otherwise she might end up spending the night in a jail cell, being held on a trumped-up charge designed to keep her close until the sheriff and Mason could figure out what was going on.

"He's going to be fine. He had a Kevlar vest under his shirt. Might have a few bruised ribs and a lot of bruised ego, but he'll recover."

"I'd still like to see him."

Mason was sure she would.

He was also sure she was hatching an escape plan, trying to come up with a way to keep herself out of the sheriff's office. That could mean she had something to hide or it could mean she was afraid.

"Good idea," he said, and she stumbled.

He tightened his grip, his hand curved around her narrow waist. She was small but muscular and he figured she could move fast if she needed to.

He wasn't going to chance a foot race. He could catch

her, but maybe not before she led them both into more trouble.

"You think me going to the hospital is a good idea?" she asked. From the tone of her voice, he'd say she was surprised by how quickly he'd acquiesced.

"Yes. You can get checked out, make sure you're not hypothermic."

"I'm going to the hospital to make sure the deputy is okay. Not because I need medical attention."

"I'm sure your family would want you to see a doctor." He'd shot an arrow in the dark, wondering if it would hit its mark. She seemed like the kind of person who'd be all about family and friendship and love. He wasn't sure what it was about her that made him think that. Maybe her story about traveling six hundred miles to help a friend.

"What do you know about my family?"

She stopped short and looked him straight in the eyes, and he knew he'd been right. She *was* all about family.

"Not much. Yet."

"What's that supposed to mean?"

"You told me a story about why you're here. It makes sense for me to check it out." He took her arm again, leading her back toward his house.

"By checking out my family?"

"Why not?"

"Because my family has nothing to do with this. If you want to confirm my story, call Bryn Laurel. She'll tell you about Henry's diagnosis. She'll explain how upset she's been, how desperate to give Henry some kind of ho—"

"We can discuss it at the hospital," he cut in. He wouldn't ask again, wouldn't let her give him more of an explanation. Not about the woman with the son who had cancer.

He could imagine the mother.

He could imagine the kid.

He could imagine getting pulled into their tragedy, and he didn't want it to happen. He'd been down that road before and it had nearly broken him. He'd seen a lot during his time in the army. He'd said goodbye to way too many comrades, but the hardest thing he'd ever done was watch his daughter suffer and then die.

Ten years ago, but it still hurt.

His relationship with his ex-wife, Felicia, hadn't survived. They'd been too different. He knew that now. Then? They'd been high school sweethearts, and he'd been joining the army. Marrying her had seemed like the right thing at the right time.

Until it wasn't.

Until months of separation and countless arguments and a beautiful baby girl who was suddenly sick and dying and gone.

He was a different man now. Older. Hopefully smarter. The past couldn't be changed, though, and he couldn't go back and offer Felicia the support he should have given her. He couldn't try to grieve with her instead of leaving her to grieve alone. He wasn't sure that would have saved the marriage. Felicia had been seeing someone else for months before their daughter's diagnosis. Maybe, though, it would have helped him move on without the boatload of guilt he carried.

Another lifetime, and not something he thought about much, but it was there—a backdrop to every decision he made.

He'd file away the information Trinity had provided. He'd check into her story, but he had no intention of contacting Bryn to ask about her son or to listen to the story of her heartbreak.

"No more questions?" Trinity asked. Her teeth weren't chattering and she'd stopped shaking. He'd like to think that was because she was warming up. They were nearly jogging along a deer trail that wound its way through the woods and out onto his property. It was more likely that she really *was* hypothermic.

"I have plenty of questions," he responded. "Now isn't the time to ask them."

"You know what my father always says?" she replied, her words slurred. She was slowing down, her gait uneven.

"What?"

"There's no time like the present."

"For asking questions?" He tightened his grip on her waist, trying to steady her. She was going to crash into a tree or tumble into a bush, but she didn't seem to know it.

"For anything."

They'd reached the edge of the forest and he could see the side of the house, the workshop where he met with clients and fitted prosthetics. An outsider would believe that he did all of his work there—computer programs and office work, designing and crafting.

That was the way he'd wanted it because his clients deserved and needed their privacy. The men who'd broken into his house had known the computer system was hidden away. They'd known about the office. They hadn't known how to access it. Mason assumed that was because he'd changed the password after John had left, but there were other possibilities. Several of his employees knew about the office. Two were able to access it. He trusted them, but he'd trusted John, too.

A group of men stood near the corner of the house and he moved toward them, Trinity stumbling along beside him.

"You need a blanket," he muttered.

"That would be nice," she said. "A blanket. A fireplace. A hot cup of tea."

"I'm not sure about the fireplace, but the hospital should be able to provide the rest."

"About that," she responded, swaying a little as she pulled away, "I've been thinking—"

"No."

"You don't know what I planned to say."

"Sure I do. You were going to say you've decided not to go to the hospital."

They'd reached the group of men. Three deputies, a state trooper and a guy who looked like a federal agent—overcoat, suit, tie, gleaming dress shoes.

He stepped away from the others. "Mason Gains?"

"That's right."

"I'm Special Agent Liam Michaels." He offered a hand and a firm shake, his gaze shifting from Mason to Trinity. "And you're…?"

"Cold," she answered, surprising a laugh out of Mason.

Agent Michaels didn't look amused. "Your name, ma'am?"

"Trinity. Miller."

"Miller?"

"Yes." She glanced past him and Mason was certain she was looking for an escape route.

"Any relation to Jackson Miller?"

"I'm his sister."

"Does he know you're here?"

"Probably not." She sidled past the agent, moved beyond the group of law enforcement officers. Mason didn't know where she thought she was going, but he followed. So did Agent Michaels.

"Would you like me to call him?" Michaels asked, shrugging out of his overcoat and dropping it around her shoulders. It was longer than the coat Mason had leant her, falling nearly to her ankles.

"Are you a friend of his?" She sidestepped the question but kept the coat, pulling it closed around Mason's.

"We've worked on a few cases together. He's a good guy."

"Yes. He is." She was heading toward the front of the house and Mason took her arm, tugging her in the other direction. "The ambulance is on the access road."

"My Jeep is around front."

"You're going to the hospital, remember?"

"Yes, but I thought I'd drive there."

"That's probably not a good idea," Agent Michaels said. "Someone attempted to kidnap you. We don't want to give him another chance."

"Is that why you're here?" Mason asked, because a federal agent didn't just happen upon little towns like Whisper. They didn't appear every time there was a gunfight or a break-in

"Yes," Agent Michaels responded.

A lie.

Mason knew it, but he wasn't going to point it out and he wasn't going to ask more questions. Not in front of Trinity. If she was as innocent as she claimed then the less she knew, the better.

An EMT jogged toward them, a pile of blankets in her arms. She handed one to Mason, then wrapped Trinity in another. "Not a good night to go for a swim, huh?" she said. "How about we get you on the ambulance and start warming you up?"

Trinity allowed herself to be led away.

Mason planned to follow but Agent Michaels stepped in front of him.

"You know who that is, right?"

"A lady who trespassed on my property."

"Her brothers own HEART."

"Should I know what HEART is?"

"A hostage extraction and rescue team. Probably the best privately owned one in the country."

"And?"

"They're not going to be happy when they find out she's involved in this."

"Care to tell me what *this* is?"

"That's what I'm here to find out, Mr. Gains."

Mason was pretty certain it was about Tate. He couldn't think of any other reason for the feds to be involved. He could have hashed it out with Agent Michaels, but he wasn't going to let Trinity leave without him. He had a few more questions to ask, and he wasn't going to let her leave before he got the chance.

"How about we discuss it at the hospital?" he asked, tossing the words over his shoulder as he jogged to the ambulance. The EMT was climbing aboard and she frowned when he stepped up beside her.

"I'm sorry, sir—"

"I'm worried about Trinity," he said. "Her family isn't around and I'm all she has." Not quite the truth. There were a couple dozen law-enforcement officers around and any one of them could have traveled to the hospital with her. He *was* worried, though.

He had no obligation to get her out of the mess she was in, but he felt an obligation to the truth and to keeping her safe. At least until her family arrived.

"Fine. You can ride along." The EMT motioned for him to climb aboard.

He found a seat next to the gurney Trinity was perched on. She'd pulled the blanket tight around her, tucked her feet up under it and covered her head. The only thing showing was her face—pale, pretty and worn. She had dark blue eyes. Something he hadn't been able to see before. Tiny lines fanned out from their corners, and he thought she might be a few years older than he'd thought. Late twenties rather than early. Someone who spent time outdoors.

And who still looked nearly frozen.

"I need to give you back your coat," she mumbled, but she didn't make any move to do it.

"I think you need it more than I do right now."

"Your pants are soaked. You've got to be cold."

"I have a blanket."

"Maybe you should go back to your house and change into something warmer."

"Trying to get rid of me?"

"Yes," she admitted, surprising him.

"Sorry to disappoint you. I'm sticking around to make sure you get to the hospital alive and to make sure you stay alive once you arrive."

"And to ask me a bunch of questions that I've already answered."

"Maybe," he admitted.

"My answers won't change. No matter how many times the questions are asked."

"The fact that you don't want me to stick around isn't going to change the fact that I'm going to," he responded, and she offered a small curve of the lips that almost passed for a smile.

"You're funny, Mason. I wouldn't have guessed that from the research I did."

"Research?" He tensed, but she didn't seem bothered by the question or the information that she'd let slip.

"I'm an internet research specialist. I can find almost anything about anyone. Once I realized what was happening to Henry, I started researching. Your name was the first to pop up in the search engine. So, of course, I had to find out more."

"Of course," he said dryly.

"You wanted honesty, Mason. I'm giving it. Now how about you give me a little space."

That wasn't going to happen, but she'd closed her eyes and leaned her head against her up-drawn knees. He figured she was trying to close him out and keep him from asking more questions. He'd let her have her way. The more time he spent with her, the more convinced he was that she was telling the truth about her friend.

Bryn Laurel and Henry.

He could almost picture them if he let himself.

He didn't.

He had other things to focus on and bigger problems to deal with.

He'd escort Trinity to the hospital, ask her a couple questions about what she'd seen, and wait for her family to arrive. He felt confident they would. Jackson Miller wasn't a name he knew, but if the FBI was aware of him, the guy had to be somebody important, his hostage rescue organization well-connected and aboveboard.

A guy like that could take care of whatever trouble might come Trinity's way, and Mason could go back to the house, do a little research of his own and find out who had the most to gain from locating Tate Whitman.

FIVE

The way Trinity figured things, she had a couple of hours before one or both of her brothers descended on Whisper Lake Medical Center and dragged her back to Maryland.

She glanced at the clock on the wall and then frowned. She'd been at the clinic for nearly three hours. First, waiting to be examined. Then, waiting for MRI results. She'd gotten the all-clear three minutes ago. It had been delivered by a nurse who'd also delivered some borrowed clothes she thought Trinity could use.

Thought?

She'd known.

All of Trinity's clothes had been bagged and tagged and sent to a forensic lab. Mason's coat had been taken, too. She'd been hanging around the hospital in nothing but a huge cotton gown, a blanket and Agent Michaels's coat.

It wasn't a good look, so she was glad for the clothes.

Plus, hospital gowns weren't exactly warm and she wanted warmth. Desperately.

She also wanted to be cleaned up, dressed and smiling before one of her brothers showed up. Otherwise her family would worry, and worrying them was top on her list of things she didn't want to do.

Seeing Mason again was at the top of her list of things

she *did* want to do, but he'd disappeared right after she'd been wheeled into the triage room. She hadn't seen or heard from him since. She'd been telling herself that was a good thing. He and the sheriff were busy following up on leads and trying to figure out who'd been in Mason's house. If they weren't questioning her, they must believe her story. If they believed her story, then she wasn't destined to spend a night in the local jail.

Not that her brothers would have let that happen, but after a pretty miserable Christmas, a lackluster New Year's celebration and a couple of months spent trying to figure out what she wanted to be now that she wasn't part of a couple, a night in jail would have seemed like the mud icing on top of the dirt cupcake that was her life.

She scowled, grabbing the pile of clothes. Oversize sweatpants, huge T-shirt with a picture of a kitten, thick socks. Shoes that were about three sizes too big. She dressed quickly, her hands still nearly frozen, her toes purple.

The doctor had said she wouldn't have any permanent damage. She didn't have a concussion, hadn't needed stitches and should be as good as new by morning.

That was great, because by morning she planned to be tucked away in the bed-and-breakfast room she'd rented for the weekend. Brothers or not, trouble or not, she planned to do what she'd set out to do when she'd left home—find purpose and excitement and renewed hope. This trip hadn't just been for Bryn. It was for Trinity, too. She needed to regroup, and she couldn't do that with her entire family hovering around, worrying that she was going to fall apart because she and Dale had broken up.

Actually, she'd broken up with Dale.

She'd told her family it was mutual.

She wasn't sure why.

Maybe because she'd thought that would be easier for them to understand and accept. After all, Trinity had been singing Dale's praises for years. Even when he hadn't deserved it. Even when she'd wondered if he was really as committed to her as she was to him.

You aren't committed to me, Trinity. You're committed to the idea of a marriage. It had been three months but she could hear Dale's words like he'd just spoken them. She could hear the accusation in his voice and she could feel the truth in her heart.

He'd been right.

She hadn't denied it then and she couldn't deny it now. That didn't change the fact that what he'd done had been wrong. It didn't change the hurt, either.

"Enough," she muttered, grabbing Agent Michaels's coat from the chair that sat near a lone window. She pulled it on over the too big clothes and walked to a metal counter and sink. No mirror, but she could see herself in the stainless-steel paper-towel dispenser.

She looked like a hot mess. Scratches on her cheeks. A bruise on her head. Dried blood in her hair. She wet a paper towel and dabbed at the areas, removing as much blood and grime as she could. She didn't have a brush, so she ran her fingers through her hair, frowning as bits of leaves and pine needles fell out.

She needed a shower.

She needed to see Mason once more.

She'd promised Bryn that she'd give it her best effort. She'd assured her that she'd do everything she could to get Mason to agree to make Henry's prosthesis. She'd kissed her friend's cheek, told her everything was going to be just fine, and she'd driven away knowing it might not be. That it probably wouldn't be. Henry was going to lose his leg. There was no doubt about that. There was a chance he would lose his life.

The thought left her cold. She couldn't treat Henry's cancer. She couldn't cure it. She wasn't a research scientist or a medical expert. She was a woman who'd spent the past few years working in an office, researching people and places, making phone calls, doing some computer forensics but mostly providing office support for her brothers' high-stress, high-risk business.

"But you promised anyway," she muttered. "Because, that's what you do. Pretend that you can fix things that only God can. Pretend you have control over things you have absolutely no control over."

"Everything okay in there?" a man called from the other side of the door.

Mason.

It had to be.

And he was just the person she wanted to see. Just the person she *needed* to see. She didn't have the power to change the course of Henry's surgery and recovery, but Mason had the ability to make at least the latter easier for the young boy. She'd give it one last shot; do everything she could to convince him to help out. If he still refused, she'd call Bryn and give her the bad news. Then she'd find a ride to the bed-and-breakfast with its cute little room and beautiful view of the lake and she'd wait for her brothers there.

"Trinity?" Mason knocked. "You okay?"

"Fine." She yanked open the door, saw him standing right at the threshold—larger than life, broader and taller than she remembered. Dark hair. Dark eyes. Hard jaw and harder expression.

He didn't look happy.

That was fine.

She wasn't happy, either.

"I thought I heard someone talking," he said, stepping into the room without an invitation, scanning the small triage area.

"I was talking to myself," she admitted, and his dark gaze settled on her face.

"About?"

"Life."

He cracked a smile. At least, she thought it was a smile.

"Do you do that often?"

"Only when there's no one else around to talk to."

"I'm around."

"You were in the hall," she pointed out, refusing to look away from his intense gaze. His eyes were the darkest brown she'd ever seen, the irises nearly as dark as the pupils. He'd changed out of his wet clothes and into a flannel shirt and faded jeans. Both clung to long, lean muscles. "Or, did you go home to change?"

"Judah drove my truck over. I had some clothes in it."

"Always prepared, huh?" she asked, unsettled in a way she didn't like. She was good with people. She always had been. She made friends easily. She kept them. She knew how to have conversations with people of all ages and she'd never had any trouble at all looking someone in the eyes. But, with Mason, she had to keep fighting the urge to look away.

"I spent the night in Nyack, New York, attending a friend's funeral. I packed a few extra changes of clothes. In case I decided to stay longer. They were still in a duffel in the truck." He watched her as he spoke, his attention never wavering.

"I'm sorry for your loss," she said, because it was the expected thing. She had no idea who his friend was, how close they were, or why he'd shared that piece of information, but she had the feeling Mason had reasons for everything he did.

"Me, too. John and I go way back."

"John Roache?" she asked and regretted it immediately.

Mason's gaze sharpened, his jaw tightening a fraction as he took a step closer. He was in her space, so close she could see the fine lines at the corners of his eyes.

Not smile lines.

She was pretty certain of that.

"What do you know about John?" he asked.

"He was your partner. The two of you developed the computer technology that you use to create prosthetics."

"John and I parted ways several years ago, so I'm wondering why you know his name."

"I told you. I did my research before I came out here. I like to know what I'm getting into before I get into it." She busied herself folding and refolding her discarded hospital gown because she was done looking into Mason's dark eyes and trying to read his implacable expression.

"If you'd done your research, you'd have realized that I only work with veterans."

"I did realize that."

"But you came anyway?"

"Wouldn't you have? If it was someone you loved?"

"Probably."

"Probably?" She swung around to face him again. "You know you would."

"You're right. I would. And I'm sorry that you did, and that you've wasted your time doing it."

"If you agreed to help, you wouldn't have to be."

He scowled. "I don't work with kids."

"You *haven't* worked with kids," she countered. "That doesn't mean you can't."

"Yeah. It does."

"Why?"

"I have my reasons."

"If you explained, maybe we could both walk away and feel good about things."

"Walk away? Is that what you think you're going to do?" he asked.

"I'm certainly not going to stick around here." She slid her feet into the too-big shoes. "And, since I don't have a ride, walking is my only option."

She really couldn't leave.

Not until someone from her family showed up.

Not unless she could find a taxi. Which might be difficult in a town the size of Whisper, Maine.

Because as much as she might be pretending that she could walk to the bed-and-breakfast, there was no way she was going to risk it. She'd been in enough danger for one night. She'd also been cold enough for a lifetime.

Yeah. She wasn't going far, but she was going, because she didn't want to look in his eyes any longer. She didn't want to say the same words over and over again and hear his same response. She'd known there was a possibility that he might refuse to help, but she hadn't wanted to think about how it would feel to tell Bryn that her hopes had been dashed.

Now she had to think about it, and thinking about it made her eyes burn and her chest tight. She wasn't a crier. If she had been, she might have let the tears fall. She loved Bryn and Henry like she loved her family. The thought of disappointing them left her hollow and empty.

Mason didn't say a word as she headed out the door. The hallway was empty, the muted sounds of machinery pulsing beneath the stillness. Her borrowed shoes squeaked as she walked to the end of the hall, her thawing toes aching every time she took a step.

She made it to the end of the corridor before Mason stopped her. He didn't put a hand on her. Didn't tell her to stop. Didn't remind her that she was part of a criminal investigation and that she couldn't leave. She could have ignored any of those things.

"They think you're my girlfriend," he said instead, and she turned, the movement so sharp she nearly toppled over.

He did grab her arm then, his grip just firm enough to steady her.

"What did you say?" she demanded, looking up into those dark eyes again.

"They think you're my girlfriend."

"Who? The FBI? The police?"

"The guys who broke into my house."

"Why would they think that?"

"I thought maybe you could answer that question."

"I can't." She started walking again, her steps as quick and brisk as she could make them with her feet flopping around in the shoes.

She wanted to pretend Mason's words hadn't changed things, but she couldn't. She'd spent enough time with her brothers and had worked enough hours at HEART to know that mistaken identity could get a person kidnapped or killed. Or both.

She grimaced, pushing through the double-wide doors that opened into a small waiting area. Like the hallway, it was empty, chairs and potted plants the only things filling the room.

"You can't run away from your troubles, Trinity," Mason said, stepping in front of her and blocking the path to the exit.

"Maybe not, but I sure can try," she responded, ducking past Mason, her heart hammering crazily in her chest.

"Where are you planning to run?" he asked, following her outside.

"Telling you that would defeat the purpose of going into hiding." She eyed the nearly empty parking lot, the few vehicles glistening with ice and rain. Beyond the exterior building lights, the night was pitch-black, the soft splatter of rain on pavement and car roofs the only sound. There were lights in the distance. House lights. Streetlights. The little town the ambulance had sped through on its way to the clinic. The bed-and-breakfast was there on Lakeview Drive.

How hard could it be to find?

And how far of a walk would it be?

A few miles?

She could do that.

Just like you could swim across the lake?

She frowned.

It was cold. It was wet. *She* was cold. She was tired. She'd already decided it was too dangerous to try to make the trip on foot.

But the lights seemed bright and cheerful and safe.

"Hiding from me isn't going to be a possibility." Mason broke into her thoughts.

She met his eyes. "What's that supposed to mean?"

"You're either part of whatever went down tonight—"

"I'm not."

"Or you've walked into something that could cause you a lot of trouble."

"I can handle it."

"You could have died tonight," he pointed out, his voice sharp-edged with irritation. "If I hadn't come home, you probably would have."

"That's a lot of assuming you're doing, Mason." She

shivered, pulling Agent Michaels's coat closer around her shoulders.

"You think I'm wrong?"

"I think I've had enough training to give me a fighting chance."

"Against men with guns?"

She didn't respond. There wasn't much she could say. He was right. They both knew it.

"Okay. Fine," she conceded, because she knew she had no choice. At least with Mason around, she had a fighting chance of survival. "I need to get to town. Can you give me a ride?"

"Agent Michaels is going to want to speak with you."

"He can speak with me at the bed-and-breakfast as well as anywhere, right?"

"The Whisper Inn?" he asked, taking her arm and steering her toward a black pickup.

"Good guess."

"Not really. It's the only bed-and-breakfast in town." He opened the passenger door of the truck and gestured for her to climb in. "I'll take you there."

"Thanks," she said, climbing into the truck and buckling her seat belt. She'd call her brothers as soon as she reached the inn, let them know where she was and that she was fine.

Mason closed the door with a quiet click and walked around the side of the truck. She expected him to climb in and get going, but he pulled out his phone instead, texting as rain splattered on the windshield. He had to be cold, but he didn't seem to be rushing.

She guessed he wasn't in any hurry.

His house was probably still off limits. He had clothes, his phone and, she presumed, his wallet with his ID.

She had nothing. Her purse was in the Jeep. Her phone

was probably still lying in the rain and ice. All she could hope for was a kind innkeeper who'd allow her to check in without identification and a credit card.

She'd cross that bridge when she came to it.

Right now, she had to focus on what she'd come for. She'd figure everything else out once she had some time alone and access to a computer. That, at least, was cut-and-dry. She could dig up plenty of information about Mason, about what he'd been working on and who he'd been working for these past few weeks. And about his business partner. John Roache. Was it a coincidence that the guy had died, that Mason had attended his funeral and that his house had been broken into while he was gone?

It wasn't her business, but if Mason was right, if she'd walked into something that could put her in danger, she needed to know where the danger was coming from.

The monsters were out there, lurking in the darkness. Not the guys with handguns and weapons. The memories of blood and death and helplessness. Most nights, Mason could push them aside by focusing on his work, by the difference he was making in the lives of his clients. But most nights, he didn't hear gunshots echoing through the woods outside his house or see a bloodied woman trying to swim for her life.

Trinity had no idea what she'd gotten herself into.

Even Mason wasn't sure. He had a direction to look in, though, and he wanted to make sure Judah was on the same page. He sent a text to him and one to Agent Michaels, letting both know where Trinity would be and informing them that Mason planned to be with her. Until they caught the guy who'd tried to kidnap her, she wasn't safe.

Cold rain dripped down his face, slid down his neck and pooled in the hollow of his throat. The texts had been sent.

People who needed to know his plan, knew it, but he didn't get back in the truck. He needed the cold air and the freezing rain to anchor him and pull him away from the memories that had haunted him for too many years to count.

Trinity rapped on the window. He ignored her. He'd spent nearly a decade living alone. He had a few close friends and a few acquaintances, but there weren't many people that he chose to spend time with. Not because he didn't like people. It was more that he didn't want to be responsible for them. He didn't want to have other people's lives in his hands. He didn't want to feel the need to protect someone and he didn't want to feel helpless if he couldn't.

He probably should have thought about that before he'd put tracking devices in the prosthetics he made. The tiny chips sent constant feedback to his mainframe, keeping logs of an amputee's movement, balance, muscle strength. When it was time for a new prosthetic or if the current one was causing pain or inhibiting movement, Mason had all the information he needed to create a new prosthetic or to correct the old one. Of course, that little computer chip also gave him the ability to find the prosthetic and, presumably, the wearer.

He hadn't thought about how valuable that information might be.

Did Tate know his prosthetic leg could lead his enemies to him? Mason hoped so. He'd explained the microchip and he'd explained that the information was being transmitted to his computer. He'd also explained that the information was secure.

He had to keep it that way.

The truck door opened and Trinity got out.

"Are you okay?" she asked, heading around the side of the vehicle before he could tell her to get back in.

"Fine," he responded, his voice grittier and harder than he'd intended.

She didn't seem intimidated by it or by him.

"Then why are you standing out in the rain?"

"I like rain."

"Do you also like ice? Because that's what you're coated in," she responded, brushing raindrops from his cheek.

It was an unconscious gesture, without artifice or design, but he felt it down to his toes, his body responding in a way he hadn't expected and didn't want. Trinity was a stranger. Even if she wasn't, he wouldn't want any connection with her. Not on any kind of level that was more than surface.

He stepped back, catching her hand when she tried to brush ice from his shoulders. "I'm pretty good at taking care of myself, Trinity, so how about you keep your hands to yourself."

She blushed.

Even in the darkness, he could see the color in her cheeks deepen.

"Sorry. I'm used to my brothers and the guys on the team. I forgot you weren't one of them."

"I'm not," he said.

"Right. I've remembered. Now, how about we get on with what we were doing?" She nearly ran back to her seat and hopped in.

He did the same, climbing into the driver's seat and shutting the door. The cab smelled like leather, stale coffee and something flowery and light that might have been soap, shampoo or lotion. He ignored it. Just like he tried to ignore Trinity.

The last was easier said than done.

The woman could talk. A lot.

And what she wanted to talk about was her friend. Bryn

Laurel. Married young. Widowed by the war in Iraq. Hero husband who'd left her with a toddler and a broken heart, and now her son had cancer.

"It's a terrible situation," Trinity said as he reached Main Street. The town was quiet this time of year. No tourists. No bands playing at the marina. Nothing but the stillness of a sleeping community.

"Cancer makes every situation terrible," he said because Trinity had finally stopped talking and he figured she expected some sort of response from him.

"But this is two huge losses for her, Mason. First her husband and now—"

"Are you saying that her son is going to die?" he cut in.

"If the cancer hasn't spread, he has a really good chance of living a long life."

"Then she isn't losing her son. She's just losing her dreams of what he could have been."

"She's terrified she's going to lose him," she argued. "And she's worried about his mental health. He's a sprinter. Already on track to go to the US Junior Championship. Without his leg, that's not going to be possible."

"People are resilient. Kids are especially resilient. Bryn's son will be just fine without one of my prosthetics." He didn't want to do it. He sure wasn't going to offer to make the kid's prosthetic. But he couldn't help thinking about his daughter, about three-year-old Amelie telling him that when she grew up, she wanted to be a princess with long, pretty hair.

He'd bought her a wig. A really expensive one that they couldn't afford—long blond hair that didn't match Amelie's tan skin and brown eyes. Felicia had hated it. She'd been angry about the expenditure and unhappy that it didn't reflect Amelie's heritage. Amelie hadn't cared about any of that. She'd loved the wig. She'd worn it everywhere. Church. The park. Preschool. Chemotherapy appointments. Hospital visits.

"I'm not asking you to do anything but meet with them," she countered. "Give Henry a little hope that he can continue running track. Give Bryn the assurance that she's doing everything she can for her son."

"She *is* doing everything she can for him. She needs to know that regardless of what I decide."

"That means you haven't made your decision, yet!" she crowed. "Which means you may still agree. Which is great. I have pictures of Henry wearing his track medals. When you see them—"

"Don't get your hopes up, Trinity. And don't get your friend's hopes up, either."

"We all need hope," she retorted. "There's nothing wrong with having it."

"When it comes to something like this, there is." He turned onto Lakeview Drive, slowing his speed as he neared the long driveway that led to the Whisper Inn. Several of his clients had stayed there, so he knew how sharp the turn was and how narrow the spruce-lined drive. There wasn't much room for error. If a car came up from behind him, he'd have nowhere to go but straight ahead. Nowhere to hide if bullets flew.

He frowned, glancing in the review mirror and probing the dark shadows. He needed to ask Annie Matlow to put up some streetlights, to illuminate the driveway a little more than it was. Annie had been innkeeper for two years. She was still learning the ropes and growing the business she'd inherited from her aunt, Lila Windhammer—Whisper Lake's most ornery resident. At least, that's what Judah said. Mason had always liked the elderly woman. Sure she'd been set in her ways and stubborn as a mule, but Mason had always appreciated that.

He'd also appreciated that she'd never tried to bring him a meal or to drag him to church. Something that just about every other elderly resident had done.

The driveway curved around a natural rock wall, the woods to one side and nothing but granite to the other. From there, it sloped up and opened into a circular parking area.

"Wow!" Trinity breathed as the house came into view. Large and stately, the Tudor-style mansion had been built over a century ago, every stone in its facade taken from a local quarry.

"It's impressive," he agreed, pulling up close to the cement stairs that led to the double-wide door.

"That's an understatement." She grabbed the door handle and would have opened it, but he reached across and grabbed her wrist, holding her in place.

"Don't."

"Get out?"

"Take needless chances. I'll go make sure the door is unlocked before you get out."

"You don't really think someone is hiding out in the woods, ready to take a potshot at me, do you?"

"No. I think someone might be waiting to get another chance at abducting you," he said.

She looked like she wanted to argue.

She looked like she had plenty to say but, instead of speaking, she crossed her arms over her chest and scowled. "Fine. We'll do it your way."

"I'm glad you see the value of that."

"What I see is that I'm tired. I have no phone. No money. No ID. I'm just hoping the innkeeper lets me check in anyway, because I don't even have a vehicle to spend the night in."

"If Annie won't let you check in, I'll make sure you

have a place to stay," he offered, the words rolling off his tongue before he thought them through.

"That's nice of you, Mason, but I didn't come here because I needed your help. I came because my friend does." She said it so sweetly he almost didn't catch the edge in her voice or see the sharpness in her eyes.

Almost didn't.

But they were there, and he wasn't one to miss much when it came to reading other people.

"No need to be bitter because I said no."

"You didn't say no."

"Sure I did."

"That was before you knew all the details."

He shrugged and got out of the truck. The night was as quiet as he'd expected it to be. The soft patter of rain and ice a rhythmic melody that could have lulled him to sleep if he were home. He jogged up the granite steps, the wrought-iron handrails shimmering with a layer of ice. He checked the front door, wasn't surprised when it opened. Annie might be new to the bed-and-breakfast, but she'd worked in the hotel industry for five years before she'd inherited Whisper Inn.

He turned back toward the truck, had barely taken a step, when Trinity exited the vehicle.

"You were supposed to wait," he snapped as she sprinted up the stairs.

"For what purpose? The door is unlocked and—"

A car engine broke through the quiet, the rumbling purr making Mason's blood run cold.

The visitor could be anybody—another guest, Judah, Agent Michaels—but Mason wasn't prepared to take chances.

"Inside, and stay there," he said, snagging Trinity's

wrist, dragging her the rest of the way to the door and giving her a gentle nudge inside.

He shut the door and sprinted down the stairs. The darkness was deepest near the edge of the woods, and he went there, slipping in between towering sweet gum trees and waiting for the vehicle to arrive.

SIX

The way Trinity saw things, she had two options. Stay inside and hope that Mason was okay or find a back door and head outside.

She knew what she should probably do.

Stay put.

So, of course, she walked through the huge entryway, moving past an ornately carved wooden staircase and into what looked like a sitting room. There were beautiful Victorian couches and gorgeous paintings. A gleaming coffee table held an arrangement of fresh flowers and several pamphlets that probably gave information about the area.

She didn't have time to look.

She wasn't looking for the innkeeper, either.

She needed a back exit and a dark path to the front of the house. Staying in the house was safe, but she couldn't let Mason face whatever was coming alone.

*Who*ever was coming.

It could be anyone. Friend or foe.

She hurried through the sitting room and into a dining room. At the far end of the room, an open pocket door revealed an industrial kitchen with gleaming stainless-steel appliances, a huge fireplace and…

A back door!

Just what she'd been looking for.

She yanked it open and walked out onto a stone patio. Like the house, it was huge and impressive, the stones gleaming in the soft light that seeped out from the kitchen. She could make out the shadowy forms of a wooden bench swing, a fire pit, a set of wicker furniture and a huge grill with a cooking utensils hanging from little hooks on its side. She grabbed what looked like a miniature pitchfork and carried it around the side of the house, following the exterior line of the building, and waiting at the front corner. She had a good view of the circular parking area, the driveway and most of the porch. It looked empty.

She eased around the corner just enough to get a view of Mason's truck. If he was in it, she couldn't see him. She didn't think he'd walked inside, so he was hiding somewhere, doing what she was doing—waiting for the approaching vehicle.

It was louder now, the engine revving as it moved up the slope that led to the house. Headlights flashed into the woods, streaming between trees and illuminating the rain-drenched shrubbery. She'd always loved rain. The sound of it pattering on the roof and dripping from leaves, the scent of moist earth and green foliage.

She wasn't loving it tonight.

She was already soaked, her hair hanging limp against her nape, her sweatshirt clinging to her skin. Agent Michaels's coat protected her back, but rain seemed to find is way down the collar onto her shoulders.

She shivered, the mini-pitchfork still clutched in her hand. Not much of a weapon, because it could only be used at close range, but it was better than nothing.

The vehicle drove into sight.

Large. Dark. Maybe with tinted windows. She couldn't make out the license plate, couldn't see the driver. She wanted to get closer but the headlights swept across the ground just feet from where she was standing.

She jerked back, bumped into something hard.

Something that hadn't been behind her before.

A hand slapped over her mouth and fingers circled her wrist. She struggled against both, but couldn't free herself enough to use the weapon she was still clutching.

"This," someone whispered in her ear, "is how easily you could be kidnapped. Maybe you'll remember that the next time I tell you to stay inside."

The hands dropped away, and she was free.

She turned, realizing she was looking into Mason's flannel shirt. It took everything in her power not to slap him upside the head or to punch him in the arm. If he'd been Jackson or Chance, she would have, but he wasn't one of her brothers or a member of HEART. She'd be really smart to keep that in mind.

"What were you thinking?" she whispered. "I could have hurt you."

"With a barbecue fork?" he asked, plucking it from her hand.

"It would have been effective."

"If you'd had a chance to use it." He stepped in front of her, blocking her view of the car.

"Is it a police cruiser?" she asked.

He shook his head. "No. Not federal, either."

"Are you sure?"

"Yes."

"How—"

"Trinity, how about we wait and ask questions after we see who's arrived?"

"I don't think the guy who kidnapped me is going to stick around to be questioned."

"It's not him."

"How do you know?" She shoved herself between Mason and the house, tried to get a look at the car. She still couldn't read the license plate or see the driver.

"As soon as I realized the car was coming up to the house, I knew it wasn't him. He'd have parked where his car wouldn't be noticed and walked in. That's assuming he knew you were coming here. Did you book online?"

"I never book online. It's too easy to be traced if you leave a cyber trail."

"Do you often worry about doing that? Or about being found?"

"I worry about finding people, Mason. That's my job. Believe it or not, I'm not some dim-witted urbanite who got herself into trouble in the Maine wilderness."

"I don't think I accused you of either of those things."

"And I don't think you need to worry about anyone knowing I'm here. Only my family and Bryn know where I'm staying."

"Shh-hhh," he whispered. "The headlights went out. Engine should go off next. We'll wait and see who gets out of the car."

Seconds later the driver cut the engine.

Trinity held her breath while she waited for the driver to get out, her heart thumping loudly in her ears. She felt sick and cold and tired, and still more afraid than she'd ever been in her life.

She'd walked into something.

She had to find a way out of it.

The passenger door opened and a tall, broad man got out. The darkness hid his features, but there was something about the way he moved that made Trinity tense.

"What is it?" Mason whispered in her ear, his breath warm against her frigid skin.

She shook her head, not quite sure what she was seeing or remembering. Until the driver's door opened and another man stepped out. Just as tall but leaner. Short hair and straight posture.

Her pulse jumped. She knew who he was before he took a step, before he gestured for the other man to follow him up the stairs.

"Chance!" she called, racing around the side of the building and straight into her oldest brother's arms.

Seeing as how Trinity had called her brother's name and thrown herself into the arms of one of the men, Mason figured she was safe enough.

He also figured he should go and introduce himself.

He wasn't exactly in the mood for it.

But, then, he never was.

A hermit. That's what people in Whisper called him. That's what he'd been called in a few human interest stories that had featured his work.

He wasn't one.

Not really.

Or, maybe, not much.

He stepped from the shadows and wasn't surprised when Chance Miller's passenger pulled out a gun and pointed it at his chest. "How about you drop the weapon, buddy?" he growled.

"It's a barbecue fork," Trinity offered.

Mason smiled. She was funny. He'd give her that.

She'd also be dead if she didn't start being a little more careful. The thought was sobering and he dropped the fork, keeping his hands where they could be seen. He didn't think the guy was going to pull the trigger, but things happened when firearms and adrenaline were around.

"Are you planning to call your bodyguard off?" Mason asked, his gaze on Trinity and her brother.

"Depends on who you are," Chance responded.

"Mason Gains. He makes—" Trinity began.

"I know what he makes, sis," Chance said. "I saw the research in your apartment."

"What were you doing there?" She swung around, her hands on her hips.

"Getting you a few things I thought you might want." He pulled a phone from his pocket. "The spare you bought last year."

"I forgot about that."

"I didn't."

"How'd you know I'd need it?"

"Jackson got a call from a friend of his."

Mason guessed. "Agent Michaels?"

Chance nodded. "That's right. He called a few hours ago. A friend of mine has a private jet and he flew us out here."

"Even with a private jet, you made quick time," Mason said, a little surprised by Chance and annoyed about that. He usually read people well, but he'd have never pegged Chance Miller for someone who ran an organization like the one Agent Michaels had described. Based on that, Mason had expected Trinity's brothers to look tough, scarred, hardened. Chance wasn't any of those things. He looked like he'd stepped out of a boardroom—suit, dress shirt, tie, polished shoes that weren't so polished anymore.

"My friend owes me, so he made it happen." He didn't offer any more details.

That was fine. Mason was more concerned about getting the guy with the gun to put it away. "You think you can tell your buddy to put away his weapon?"

"My buddy is Cyrus Mitchell."

"And his buddy doesn't feel like putting away his weapon," Cyrus added. Unlike Chance, he looked like a guy who'd faced down some serious adversaries. Lean. Hard. A little edgy.

And then, there was the gun he still had pointed straight at Mason. Glock. Standard issue. Nothing fancy but it would do the job and kill a man with very little skill needed from the shooter.

At this distance, Cyrus wouldn't need skill.

One shot and it would be over.

"You should probably do it, anyway," Chance suggested. "Before law enforcement shows up. We don't want to start off on thc wrong sidc of things."

"I don't see why not," Cyrus grumbled, but he tucked the gun into its holster and eyed Mason dispassionately. "It's not cool coming out of the shadows with a weapon in your hand."

"It's not cool pulling a gun on someone who's done nothing wrong."

"It's dark. It's raining. You're moving toward us with a deadly—"

"Barbecue fork," Trinity interjected, and Chance laughed.

"Leave it to you to try and lighten the mood, sis," he said, pulling her in for another hug. "How about we move this inside?" He glanced at the house. "This is where you planned to stay, right?"

"I did tell you that before I left."

"You also told me you were up here to see the foliage and pick some apples and do some sightseeing. Obviously that was a lie." He glanced at Mason and frowned. "And, obviously, that lie almost got you killed."

"Whatever story you were told was grossly exaggerated by whoever told it."

"I got the story from Jackson who got it from Liam Michaels. I doubt a federal agent has any reason to exaggerate." He cupped Trinity's elbow and led her to the steps.

She looked even smaller standing next to her brother, her hair plastered to her head and neck, her body encased in an oversize coat and too big sweats. She'd cleaned up at the hospital. Mason had noticed that. No more blood streaked across her face or hands or caked in her hair. He'd also noticed the deep blue of her eyes, the natural highlights in her hair, the dimples in her cheeks when she smiled. She looked like a kid, and she had the sweet, easy disposition of someone who'd never faced hardship. He could understand why her brother was so protective, why he'd drop everything, call in favors and make record time to help her out of trouble.

But Mason wasn't sure she needed it as much as her brother thought. She'd managed to escape a would-be kidnapper, had been able to run away from the guys who'd been in his house and hide for long enough to have a fighting chance at survival. Maybe, like her brother, Trinity's looks were deceiving. And maybe she'd come to Maine, approached Mason, asked for help for her friend, because she'd wanted to prove she was more than what her brothers thought.

He frowned, not much liking that thought.

If she was here to prove something to her family or to her brothers, that could be a problem. She might make rash decisions, make poor choices, put herself in danger for the sake of proving something she didn't really need to prove.

Not his business.

None of this was his business.

His business was to figure out who'd sent the guys who'd broken into his place. His job was to make sure no one got their hands on his computer system. Not that it would be easy to hack into. He had plenty of firewalls in place and more than enough safety nets.

If he was dealing with the average everyday criminal.

He was worried that he wasn't.

Tate Whitman could bring a very high-ranking military official down and, more than likely, get several others tossed into military prison. Mason might enjoy his solitude, but he kept up to date on the news. He knew how big the case was and what the implications were of being the only witness to something that had cost dozens of servicemen and women their lives.

Tate had been fortunate to survive, and if he was the reason for this, if silencing him was the goal of the people who'd broken into Mason's house, Mason was going to make very sure they weren't successful.

He followed Trinity and her brother to the front door, wasn't surprised when it opened before they reached it.

Annie Matlow stood in the doorway, her short, black hair framing a face that had made every bachelor in Whisper Lake knock on her door. Even Judah had given it a try. He'd told Mason the story and laughed when he'd said that Annie had sent him packing but offered a plate of cookies as a consolation prize.

"Check-in times ended an hour ago," Annie said bluntly. "And all the noise you're making out here is disturbing my other guests."

"You have a full house?" Chance asked, his hand still on his sister's elbow.

"I have rooms. But not for people who are going to cause trouble." Her gaze jumped from Chance to Trinity. "You're Trinity Miller."

"Yes, I—"

"Ran into a little trouble. I heard. News travels fast around here. I heard you come in a few minutes ago. Would have come down then, but I was helping Mrs. Earl with a painting project."

"It's kind of late for painting, isn't it?" Cyrus asked, and

Annie scanned the group, her stunning face set in a scowl that did nothing to detract from her beauty.

"It's kind of late to arrive on someone's doorstep, too, but here you are."

"Extenuating circumstance," Chance offered.

"So I hear. I suppose you all want to come in, so let's get it over with." She turned on her heel and walked back inside.

She wasn't the type that appealed to Mason. Too Felicia-like for his taste—gorgeous and haughty, with just a hint of disdain in everything she said, but there was another side to her that Judah seemed to appreciate. A side that handed out cookies and helped with painting projects late at night.

"She's pleasant," Trinity whispered as she stepped across the threshold.

"She can be whatever she wants as long as she's willing to give me a place to sleep for a couple of hours," Cyrus responded. "I just got home yesterday."

"I know," Trinity said. "I booked your fight in and out of Madrid, remember? And I told Chance you'd need the next couple of weeks off. Apparently he didn't listen."

"Sure he did. I'm not going on mission until the end of the month."

"And yet, you're here," she pointed out.

"This isn't work, Trinity," Cyrus responded. "It's family."

She kept silent, whatever she was thinking hidden behind her pale, scratched face and her bright blue eyes.

Maybe because she wasn't sure how to respond.

Maybe because Annie had stopped in the dining room and was pointing at the large table. "Everyone sit. I've got some scones left over from breakfast. I'll make some tea and you can have some refreshments. Then we'll decide what I'm going to do about all the unexpected guests."

"No need to worry about me, Annie," Mason said. "I'm going to head back to the house as soon as everyone gets settled here."

"I'll come with you," Trinity volunteered.

Her brother frowned. "I don't think so."

"Mason and I have some unfinished business."

"No. We don't," he responded, looking straight into her gorgeous blue eyes.

She didn't look convinced. She looked…hopeful? Desperate?

"You do know that your house is a crime scene, right?" Annie asked.

"Yes."

"And you know the state crime lab van is there?"

"I figured it would be." He also figured it wouldn't take long to process the scene.

"Then you also know your chances of having a bed to sleep in tonight are slim to none. I'll plan a room for you while I get the scones."

She walked away, shoulders stiff beneath a soft blue sweater, steps quick and impatient.

"Well, that's settled, then." Trinity spoke into the silence, her voice cheerful and light, her face and lips colorless. "We'll all spend the night in this beautiful bed-and-breakfast, and in the morning, we'll sort everything out."

That wasn't going to happen.

Mason was heading home. He didn't say as much. No sense sparking off a debate or giving Trinity a heads-up. He wanted her to stay right where she was, safe in her brother's protection. He'd stick around until he made sure that was going to happen and then he'd head back to the house. It might be a fight to gain entrance with the state forensic team there, but Judah had a way of getting what he wanted, and Mason hoped he wanted to help. Mason needed to get into his office and assure himself the restricted data was secure. Once he did that, he might be able to rest.

Or, maybe, he'd figure out where Tate was and take a road trip to make sure he knew he had some people gunning for him. People who seemed willing to do just about anything to take him down.

SEVEN

A half hour after they'd arrived at Whisper Inn, Trinity had managed to choke down a scone and answer every question her brother had asked all while avoiding Mason's dark eyes.

He'd taken a seat at the end of the long, dining room table and hadn't said a word during the interrogation. Scratch that. Not an interrogation. An interview. That's what Chance would call it. Trinity wanted to call it a pain in the neck. She had nothing to offer beyond what her brother had learned from the sheriff and Agent Michaels. He'd apparently been on the phone with them several times during the course of his travels.

She wasn't surprised by that. She was tired. Cold. Ready for the night to be over and the sun to rise.

"You look beat, Trinity," Mason suddenly said, and she made the mistake of meeting his eyes.

There was something in their depths, something dark and a little lonely, that made her want to ask questions and get answers and learn all the reasons why a guy who had so much to offer chose to offer it to a limited few.

"It's been a long day."

"Driving six hundred miles will make any day long,"

Cyrus said, snagging another scone from the tray Annie had left.

"Yes," she agreed, but that wasn't the reason it had been long. She'd been excited when she'd left home, happy to be going on an adventure by herself, eager to meet Mason. Ready to find some new direction, new focus, something besides her tired dreams of doing something more than sitting in an office all day waiting for her jerk of a boyfriend to propose.

"I had Stella pack you an extra bag. Just in case," Chance said. "It's in the rental. I'll grab it and then you can go up to your room and get some sleep."

While the rest of us finish discussing things and make plans.

She could almost hear the unspoken words and had to try really hard not to resent them. Her brothers had their reasons for trying to protect her, but she had a life to live outside of the tragedy that had occurred when she was a kid.

The fact that she had just a few memories of her sister probably made it easier to move on and let go. Or it would, if her parents and brothers weren't constantly trying to micromanage her life to keep her safe.

"You know what?" she said, pushing away from the table and standing. "I'm going up to my room *now*."

"Did Annie tell you which one it is?" Mason asked. He wasn't looking at her the way her brother and Cyrus were—like she was a delicate bud that could be easily bruised.

"No, but I'll track her down and find out."

"You're upset," Chance said, grabbing her hand as she walked past.

"I'm just clearing the way for you to do what you always

do, Chance," she said, knowing she sounded as weary and frustrated as she felt.

"What's that?" He quirked a brow and looked like he had no idea what she was talking about.

He probably didn't.

She'd never told him that he was smothering her. She'd never asked him for more than a chance to prove herself as a member of the team.

"Take control of things," she said without heat because she couldn't be angry at her brother for doing what he did best.

She was just angry with herself for not figuring out her own path a little sooner. Everyone had gifts, right? Each person was handpicked for a divine purpose. She'd always believed that.

Lately, though, she couldn't quite figure out what hers was supposed to be. Not getting married and having kids. That was for sure. Not going overseas and helping to free hostages, either.

"Trin—" Chance began.

"Don't worry about it, okay? Cyrus was right. It was a long drive. I need to get some sleep." She kissed his cheek, tugged her hand from his and pasted on the brightest smile she could manage. Then she straightened her shoulders and walked from the room. She might feel useless, aimless and unsure, but she wasn't going to let anyone know that.

Annie wasn't in the sitting room or in the entrance room. She didn't respond when Trinity called her name, either. As a matter of fact, the entire place felt empty. Trinity walked through the downstairs of the immense house, her footsteps echoing hollowly in a few of the sparsely furnished rooms. It was a beautiful place, but there were signs of neglect—wallpaper peeling in spots, floor scuffed from over a century of feet moving across them. The threadbare carpet runner in the long hallway that led from the east to the west side of the house had faded years ago.

A person could disappear in a house like this one. There were dozens of places to hide—heavy velvet drapes covering floor-to-ceiling windows, dark, empty recesses that might have once contained statues. She stepped into a room that might have been a ballroom an eon ago but now served as a library, the walls lined with shelves and books. French doors led from there to the patio, the upper panels intricate stained glass. She moved closer, touching the figure of an angel.

"Pretty, huh?" someone said and it was all Trinity could do not to scream. She whirled around to find Annie standing near a bookshelf at the far end of the room.

"Where did you come from?"

"Secret passageway behind the shelves."

"No. Really. Where were you? The room was empty when I walked in."

"There *is* a secret passage behind this shelf. Actually, it's more like a servant staircase. My grandfather thought it would be funny to create a secret door and give visitors something to talk about." She pressed the center of a flower carved into the side of the shelf and the entire thing slid open soundlessly, revealing a narrow staircase beyond.

"Wow."

"Right? My family was interesting. I'll give them that." She ran a hand over her blue-black hair and smiled tiredly.

"You must love it, though."

"The inn? I'm not sure how I feel about it. The tradition of it? That, I can get behind a little more. Unfortunately my aunt wasn't a very prudent businesswoman. Things aren't looking too good for the place."

"I'm sorry."

"Don't be. I'll figure them out. You ready to head to your room?"

"Are we taking the secret passage?"

"Too many cobwebs and too much dust. Besides, your key is at the front desk."

"I didn't realize there was one."

"My aunt made certain it was well hidden. She didn't like worrying people about money, so the transactions were all done where no one could see. The office is at the top of the main stairs. You're in room 210. Right at the back of the house. Beautiful view of the lake and the lawn. It's very quiet. The men are in the three rooms right at the top of the stairs. I figured you might want a little space from them."

"How'd you guess?"

Annie shrugged. "I had two brothers a lifetime ago. They were a lot older than me. If I'd let them, they'd have smothered me with concern and love."

"You had two brothers?" Trinity asked, moving across the room.

"People die, Trinity. You look very young and very sheltered, but I'm sure you know that."

"How about you retract the claws, Annie? I haven't done anything to deserve them." Trinity wasn't in the mood to accept criticism from a complete stranger.

"Sorry." Annie grimaced. "And I mean that sincerely. I quit smoking two weeks ago and I'm not exactly fun to be around. I should have warned you when you made your reservations and suggested you find a place in the next town over. I won't charge you for the night if you want to leave in the morning. Go on upstairs. Turn right at the top. The light is on in the office and the key is right on the desk. If you need anything, let me know." She walked to the French doors and opened them, letting in wintery air that held a hint of pine and wet earth and wood-burning fires. They were homey scents at odds with the cavernous room and marble floors and the testy young woman who'd walked outside.

If Trinity had been smart, she'd have taken Annie's advice and gone to find the key, but something about the slope of the other woman's shoulders, the tired way she'd moved as she'd walked outside, reminded Trinity of Bryn. That was enough to cool her temper and make her wonder what Annie's story was, why she'd taken over an inn that she didn't really love, and what had happened to cause her brothers' deaths.

And that, of course, was enough to get her moving back across the room and out onto the patio. She scanned the area, saw Annie walking toward the bluff that looked out over the lake.

"Annie!" she called. "Hold up!"

But Annie just kept walking.

She followed, picking her way across the ran-soaked lawn, the storm blowing rain and ice into her face. Up ahead, Annie had reached the bluff and seemed to step over the edge and disappear from sight.

Terrified, Trinity sprinted forward, not sure what she would do if Annie really had gone over the edge.

But, of course, she hadn't.

There was a wide metal guardrail and a gate that opened onto a path that must go down to the lake.

Pretty, but Trinity had no desire to get close to the water again. Annie knew what she was doing. She owned the property and she obviously didn't think walking down the path during a storm was dangerous.

Trinity hoped it wasn't.

Maybe she should check. Just go down a few yards, get the lay of the land and make sure Annie hadn't tumbled over the side.

"It can't hurt," she said, reasoning aloud because she was alone in the middle of a storm. "And if Annie has gotten into any kind of trouble, I'll just call for he—"

A hand slammed over her mouth and she was yanked backward with enough force to lift her off her feet. For a split second she thought it was Mason, proving a point again, but her assailant's hand was rough, his palm so tight against her mouth, her teeth ground into her lips.

She struggled as he dragged her backward. No gun pressed to her head or chest. No threats. The guy was just yanking her along like she was a rag doll, barely giving her feet a chance to touch the ground.

Don't panic! her mind shrieked. *Think!*

She'd had all the classes. She'd trained to defend herself in situations like this. She knew what she was supposed to do, but the guy seemed to be seven feet tall and about the same width, his arms heavy with muscle, his hand smelling of alcohol, cigarette smoke and something else. Something metallic and familiar.

She couldn't place it.

Didn't have the time to think it through.

He dragged her to the woods that lined the property and his grip shifted, his muscles tightening in preparation for something. She had no idea what and she didn't give him a chance to show her.

She slammed her head into his chin with enough force to make her see stars. He yowled, losing his grip as he fell backward. She was free and she wasn't foolish enough to wait to see if he came at her again.

She took off. Feet slipping on ice-coated grass.

Please, God, let the door still be unlocked.

Please...

The rest of the prayer faded as a shadow darted toward her, moving with so much speed she didn't have time to sidestep, didn't have time to evade. She did have time to scream, the sound torn from her throat as she tried to take off in the opposite direction.

One minute she was screaming. The next she was tossed over someone's shoulder, her head banging against a hard back as the person pivoted and raced back the way he'd come.

She wanted to keep screaming but every jarring step forced the air from her lungs. Her screams were reduced to quiet, desperate gasps as she tried to shimmy away.

"It's me."

Just those two words. But she knew the voice. And she might have even known the broad hands and muscular shoulders, the warm flannel and—more than any of those—the quick, decisive action.

"Mason?" she managed to gasp.

"Yeah. So how about you stop fighting? I want to get you inside. The sooner, the better."

She couldn't agree more.

There was nothing cool or fun or exciting about being scooped up and carried like a sack of potatoes.

"Someone—"

"I saw him from the library."

"What were—"

"I was looking for you."

"Why?"

"Trinity, how about you let it rest for about five seconds?" He ground the words out and she pressed her lips together, letting her hands rest on his rib cage and back.

She wanted down.

Now.

She also didn't want to be the reason Mason got hurt.

They'd reached the patio and he sprinted across it, flew

through the French doors and dropped her onto the nearest chair.

"You going to stay put this time or do I need to get your brother involved?" he asked.

"He's already involved," Chance growled.

She turned, saw him stalking across the room, a look on his face she'd only ever seen a couple of times.

Fear mixed with anger and relief.

"Good, because I want to have a little chat with someone." Mason was out the door before anyone could speak again, disappearing into the storm so quickly he might not have been there at all.

"I can't believe you were out there, Trinity," Chance snapped, his blue eyes blazing with frustration.

"Sure you can," she responded.

Some of his anger faded away. "What were you thinking?"

"That someone needed to make sure Annie was okay. It's not like I went out there alone."

"Then what happened?"

"She headed down to the beach and when I tried to follow..." She didn't want to tell him. Not all the details. It would scare him too much. "There was someone out there, Chance."

"Trinity..." He didn't say whatever he was thinking. Just shook his head.

She refused to feel guilty for what she'd done. She wouldn't feel foolish, either. There was no way anyone could have tracked her to the inn and no reason why anyone would want to.

They think you're my girlfriend.

Mason's words rang through her head as Chance texted Cyrus. Probably asking him to come babysit Trinity.

She kept her mouth closed, refusing to tell him she didn't need to be guarded.

"Cyrus's on his way down," Chance finally said. "Do not leave this room without him."

With that, he ran out the French doors, shutting them firmly behind him.

Five minutes.

That had been the difference between danger and safety.

If Mason hadn't decided to check on Trinity one last time before he returned home… If he hadn't thought he'd heard voices coming from somewhere at the back of the house… If he hadn't walked into the library and seen the open door…

Things could have turned out a lot differently.

If there was a silver lining to the giant black cloud that seemed to be hanging over their heads, it was that the thug who'd come after Trinity didn't want her dead. What he wanted was to use her as a pawn. Of course, once she'd helped him accomplish his goal, she'd be dispensable.

Not a good thought.

Mason needed to find the guy calling the shots and paying the bills. If he could stop him, he could keep both Tate and Trinity safe.

Feet pounded on the ground behind him and splashed in the puddles the rain was leaving behind. He didn't turn around. He knew it was either Chance or Cyrus. Probably Chance. He'd want to get his hands on the guy who'd grabbed his sister. That's how Mason would have felt if he'd had siblings.

He didn't.

Since his grandfather had passed away three years ago, he didn't have anyone. That didn't bother him. But watching Chance and Trinity together had reminded him of things he'd longed for when he was kid, things he'd thought he'd have when he'd married Felicia.

Seconds later Chance sprinted up beside him. He wasn't gasping for breath. He wasn't winded. It seemed to Mason the guy could have kept that pace for a mile and not broken a sweat.

"Do you know which direction he went?" Chance asked.

"Through the trees. Over this way." He found the spot where the guy had disappeared, flashing his Maglite on the tamped-down grass and broken branches.

"You have any idea who he is?"

"No." He did have an idea who'd sent him. A vague idea, but an idea.

"Any idea what he wants with my sister?"

"I'd assume he wants to use her to manipulate me."

"You don't even know each other."

"He doesn't know that."

"Maybe you should tell him." Chance knelt near a boot print pressed into the damp ground.

"I'd do that. If I had any idea who he was."

Chance snapped a picture of the boot print and straightened. "Come on, Gains. You can't tell me that you have no idea what's going on here. You were a military guy. Well trained. You're a decorated veteran with two PhDs in fields that most people would flunk out of their first semester."

"You've done your research."

"Better than coming into a situation blind. So, what's going on? Who's after you? Why? And what does it have to do with my sister?"

"I'm not sure. On any of those questions."

"But you have an idea."

"Ideas are easy to come by, Chance."

"They're also easy to share."

"I'll tell you what I know," he said, because if he were

a brother, if his sister were in danger, he'd want as much information as he could get to help keep her safe. "After we follow this guy's trail."

"Should be easy enough to do. He wasn't being careful."

"He was panicked. Your sister head-butted him and he lost his grip. I think he thought she'd be an easy mark, and I think the fact that she wasn't flustered him."

"Head-butted?"

"Back of her head into his chin." Mason had seen it all, the guy lunging out of the shadows and grabbing Trinity, the struggle as he'd pulled her toward the woods.

Reaching her had taken seconds.

It had seemed like a dozen years.

He'd been terrified they'd disappear into the woods and he'd lose them there. She wasn't his responsibility. He knew that. But it felt like she was.

"Trinity is tougher than she looks. That played to her advantage."

"She's also smart," Mason added.

Chance glanced his way. "That goes without saying."

"That makes the fact that she was out here surprising. She can't keep making decisions that put her in harm's way. If she does, it could get her killed."

"What is it she knows or has that is worth killing her for?" Chance asked, no hint of emotion in his voice.

With anyone else, Mason would have assumed that was a good thing. He had a feeling Chance was an exception; that the calmer he sounded, the more angry he was.

"Nothing."

"Then she shouldn't be in any danger. We find the guy who's out here. We turn him in to the police. Then Cyrus, Trinity and I will hit the road and put some distance between ourselves and whatever trouble you're in."

"Good idea. In theory." Mason stepped over a fallen

tree, following a trail of broken branches and partial footprints through the woods. He could see where the guy was heading—down to the road and back toward town.

"In theory…how?"

"Somehow someone got the impression that Trinity and I are dating. That person wants information I have. If she were my girlfriend, then having her might give them something to negotiate with."

Chance didn't respond. He was probably thinking things through, trying to decide how Mason's theory impacted Trinity's safety.

It impacted it a lot.

Far be it from Mason to make that announcement.

They reached a footpath that had been paved years ago. It had probably been a shortcut from the inn to town, but it hadn't been maintained. The cement was crumbling, plants shooting up through cracks, trees and bushes crowding in on it.

"You know where this leads?" Chance asked.

"It's heading toward town, but I've never heard of anyone using it and I don't know where it dumps out."

"Is there someone local who might know? Annie, maybe? If we can figure out where this is leading, we can have the sheriff send some men to intercept the guy."

"I can call the sheriff. He's lived in Whisper Lake most of his life. Annie is new to the area." He pulled out his cell phone and was dialing as they climbed a small hill, nearly sliding down the other side. The path was clear enough and the footprints the perp had left on the icy ground were obvious.

Judah answered immediately, his voice sharp and filled with concern. "Where are you? I got a call from Trinity. She said there's been trouble at the inn. I'm en route now."

"We're on a path in the woods to the east of Whisper Inn. You happen to know where it leads?"

"Cement or dirt?"

"Cement. Old and crumbling. Looks like it's been here for a while."

"Leads to the old church on Sullivan Road. You know it?"

"Yeah."

"I'm heading in that direction. Go back to the inn. I've got a deputy heading over to take statements. I'll call when I have the guy in custody."

He disconnected and Mason shoved the phone into his pocket.

"Does he think he can head the guy off?" Chance asked.

"Probably."

"Do you think he can?"

"I don't know."

"And?"

"I'm not going to take the chance."

"So, we keep going?"

"Yeah. We do."

"How's the sheriff going to feel about that?"

"I guess I'm going to find out. Feel free to go back to the inn if you're worried about getting into trouble with local law enforcement."

"I'm more afraid of letting this guy get away," Chance responded as something flashed on the path in front of them.

A flashlight maybe. There. Gone. There again.

A signal of some sort?

Was it possible the perp wasn't alone?

"I don't like this," Chance muttered, but he was still moving forward, silently and quickly.

Mason was right beside him, his body humming with

adrenaline, his muscles taut with it. He wanted this guy caught as badly as Chance did.

They reached the edge of the forested area and the path wound through an open field. Just beyond it, Mason could see the church, its siding white in the darkness, its steeple straight and elegant.

He was surprised at how stately it looked—darkness nearly hiding the boarded-up windows, the spray-painted front door. Years ago, the building had been abandoned when the church moved closer to town. Since then, it had been empty. When Mason had first moved to Whisper Lake, there'd been a For Sale sign sitting in the churchyard, faded and worn from too many years being out in the elements. It had disappeared sometime in the last couple of years. Maybe taken by one of the teens who liked to meet in the churchyard to party or tell ghost stories or attempt to get into the old building.

He scanned the area, looking for signs of the perp. The guy had been moving at a quick clip. He either knew the area well or he'd spent time getting the lay of the land. Considering how quickly things were moving, Mason was leaning toward the first scenario.

"See anything?" Chance asked, his voice barely carrying over the rain and the wind.

"Nothing that makes me want to go exploring."

"What's on the other side of the building?"

"About the same as what you see on this side."

"How about we split up, then? You head around the front. I'll head around the back. We'll see if we can head the guy off. You have a gun?"

"No."

"I won't ask if you know how to use one. You were military." Chance reached under his coat and pulled out a handgun. "It's loaded. Safety is on," he said as he handed it to Mason. "I'll meet you around the other side of the church. Whistle if you spot the perp. Try not to engage in a gun battle. We want him alive. I have a lot of questions I'd like to ask."

So did Mason.

He moved away, skirting the edge of the overgrown yard and then cutting across the crumbling parking lot. He planned to go straight to the other side of the building, but something caught his attention. A hint of movement in his periphery. He dove for cover, sliding across the icy ground and scrambling behind bushes that butted up against the facade of the church.

He probed the darkness, spotting the movement again. In the yard. Close to the road. It looked like fabric fluttering in the breeze. He flashed his Maglite toward it, caught the movement in its beam—cloth fluttering, a pale hand. Dark hair. A dark stain beneath a still body.

Blood. Mixing with the rain and the ice, puddling on the broken pavement. His mind flashed back ten years. His fiftieth helicopter flight. Racing from the scene of an IED explosion to the trauma team waiting at their military outpost, three young soldiers hovering between life and death.

For a moment he was frozen, caught between two worlds, two times, memories of what had been and the reality of what was.

Then he was moving, all the old training kicking in as he raced across the lot and knelt beside the fallen man.

EIGHT

She should have stayed at the inn.

That would have been the safe thing to do. It might even have been the prudent thing to do, but it had only taken Trinity three minutes on the internet to figure out the best place for a person to park if he wanted to walk to the inn. It had taken her ten minutes longer to convince Cyrus to drive her to the location. Three miles by car. Less than one through the woods. If the perp had done what she thought he had—parked far enough away not to be heard—they might be able to head him off before he escaped.

She'd told Cyrus that, and then she'd told him that she planned to go to Whisper Lake Community Church with or without him. If she didn't have a ride, she'd find one. Of course, he knew she didn't have a ride, and he knew there wasn't a ride to be found anywhere in the vicinity. He probably still would have refused if Annie hadn't returned to the inn, heard the discussion and offered to lend her car.

That had been enough to get Cyrus to concede defeat.

He'd taken the keys to Annie's beat-up Cadillac Seville, muttering under his breath as Trinity had shrugged into her borrowed coat and walked outside.

Now they were less than a mile from the church, the old country road shiny and slick, the sky an odd gray-black. She'd been in this part of the country when she was a kid, traveling with her parents to a campground on a lake. She couldn't remember the name of the lake or the campground, but she could remember the sky in the summer—clear azure blue—the feel of the cold water and the gravely bottom of the lake.

This part of Maine was nothing like she remembered. It was cold, austere and dangerous.

Or, maybe, she felt that way because of everything that had happened since she'd arrived.

She glanced at her cell phone, eyeing the direction to the church. "We're less than a half mile away. You might want to kill the lights."

Cyrus grunted but did as she'd suggested. "If I get fired for this," he growled, "you can explain it to my wife."

"You're not going to get fired."

"Tell that to your brother when he finds out I let you talk me into this."

"You came to protect me, because I was coming with or without you. That's our story. We're sticking with it. No matter what my brother says."

"Right. Sounds good. We'll see if your brother buys it. *If* we ever get to the church." He'd slowed the Cadillac to a crawl, the dark road and blowing rain making visibility difficult.

"We will," she reassured him, but she wasn't nearly as confident as she sounded. She was good at certain things. Finding information was one of them. Breaking into computer systems was another.

Her sense of direction, though…

That left a lot to be desired.

But she was using Google Maps.

That should get them where they needed to be.

Except that she was beginning to think that where they

needed to be was back at the inn. It wasn't that she was afraid of the weather, the dark road or her brother. But the uneasy feeling she'd had earlier, the one that she'd ignored, had returned. She felt it at the back of her skull, nudging at her mind, warning her that something wasn't right.

"I think you should pull over," she said, her heart hammering in her chest.

"Find a place and I will," he responded.

He was right.

There was no place to pull over. Nothing but fields of uncut hay, copses of trees, gnarly bushes and the darkness. Anything could be hiding there.

Or anyone.

"What's wrong?" Cyrus said quietly, all the annoyance gone from his voice.

"Just a feeling."

"What kind of feeling?"

"One that's telling me that we shouldn't be here. Not right now." She felt silly saying it, but Cyrus nodded.

"I've got the same one. But, look..." He gestured to their left and she could see an old church that stood on a gentle knoll overlooking the road. "That must be the church we've been searching for. Your brother is already there."

"How do you know?"

"I texted him before we left the inn."

Of course he had.

Of course he couldn't do what Trinity wanted without checking with one of her brothers.

That's the way everyone at HEART was.

"You didn't tell me that before we left."

"And you didn't tell him that you planned to leave. Maybe we both should have been more forthcoming."

"And maybe the reason we both have a bad feeling about

this place is because we can feel the wrath of my brother swirling through the stormy air."

"Nice imagery, Trinity, but I don't think it's that." He glanced in his review mirror and frowned. "Looks like the local police have arrived."

She glanced back, saw emergency lights flashing in the distance. "Did you call them, too?"

"Your brother must have. Or Mason."

Mason?

She'd been trying not to think about him or the way he'd tossed her over his shoulder and carried her to safety.

Not that it had been romantic or thrilling or in any way a moment she wanted to repeat. No. Humiliating was more the word she'd put with it.

Cyrus managed to find the church parking lot and turned into it, bouncing over a few speed bumps as he made his way toward the old building.

He still had his lights off and Trinity still had the feeling they shouldn't be there. Maybe it was the creepiness of the church with its boarded-up windows and vandalized door. Maybe it was the way the wind was whipping the old elm tree that stood in the center of the churchyard. Whatever the case, she felt uneasy, anxious, a little scared.

"Did my brother say where he was going to be?" she asked as Cyrus parked the Cadillac. "I'm surprised he's not standing here waiting to lecture me."

"He said the parking lot. That's where we are, so how about we stay put and—"

He said more but she didn't hear. She'd spotted something in the churchyard—a dark figure hunched over in the long grass.

Cyrus must have seen it, too. He'd gone silent, was pulling out his gun. "Stay here," he said as he got of the Cadillac and slammed the door.

READER SERVICE—**Here's how it works:**

Accepting your 2 free Love Inspired® Suspense books and 2 free gifts (gifts valued at approximately $10.00) places you under no obligation to buy anything. You may keep the books and gifts and return the shipping statement marked "cancel." If you do not cancel, about a month later we'll send you 6 additional books and bill you just $5.24 each for the regular-print edition or $5.74 each for the larger-print edition in the U.S. or $5.74 each for the regular-print edition or $6.24 each for the larger-print edition in Canada. That is a savings of at least 13% off the cover price. It's quite a bargain! Shipping and handling is just 50¢ per book in the U.S. and 75¢ per book in Canada.* You may cancel at any time, but if you choose to continue, every month we'll send you 6 more books, which you may either purchase at the discount price plus shipping and handling or return to us and cancel your subscription. *Terms and prices subject to change without notice. Prices do not include applicable taxes. Sales tax applicable in N.Y. Canadian residents will be charged applicable taxes. Offer not valid in Quebec. Books received may not be as shown. All orders subject to approval. Credit or debit balances in a customer's account(s) may be offset by any other outstanding balance owed by or to the customer. Please allow 4 to 6 weeks for delivery. Offer available while quantities last.

If offer card is missing write to: Reader Service, P.O. Box 1867, Buffalo, NY 14240-1867 or visit www.ReaderService.com

NO POSTAGE
NECESSARY
IF MAILED
IN THE
UNITED STATES

BUSINESS REPLY MAIL

FIRST-CLASS MAIL PERMIT NO. 717 BUFFALO, NY

POSTAGE WILL BE PAID BY ADDRESSEE

READER SERVICE
PO BOX 1867
BUFFALO NY 14240-9952

She watched as he walked toward the figure, heard a muffled shout, and was surprised when Cyrus holstered his weapon. Another muffled shout and he ran toward the hunched figure.

She hopped out of the car and followed, knowing he'd have never put his gun away if he thought there was danger.

She reached his side in seconds, was a few feet away from the hunched figure when she realized what she was seeing. A man lying prone on the ground, blood staining the ground beneath him. Chance was to one side of him, trying to staunch the flow from a wound in the guy's stomach.

Mason was doing chest compressions, trying to pump whatever blood remained back to the guy's heart.

"What happened?" she asked, dropping down beside him and feeling for a pulse. Nothing.

"That's a question we'll only get an answer to if this guy lives," Chance responded, his voice tight with worry.

"Twenty-one-and-two-and-three-and-four." Mason counted compressions aloud, ignoring Trinity, Cyrus and Chance, his focus on the man he was trying to help.

A young man.

Trinity could see that as she leaned close, listened for breath sounds. "Did you check his airway?"

"Yes," Chance said. "It's clear."

"Nine-ten," Mason continued, stopping compressions, feeling for the pulse. "Still nothing," he said grimly.

"I'll breathe," Trinity offered, leaning in, blowing two quick breaths into the guy's lungs.

She saw his chest rise and fall, felt for a pulse again.

They worked like that as vehicles pulled into the church lot and men and women climbed out of marked cars and ambulances. Trinity was only partially aware of the activity. Her focus was on the man who lay lifeless on the cold grass.

When someone tried to nudge in beside her, she stayed put. Would have kept right on working if Chance hadn't grabbed her arm and hauled her away. "Let the experts take over," he said quietly. She could hear the sadness in his voice and knew what he was thinking.

"Who is he?" she asked because she could imagine a mother or father or wife or girlfriend being given the news that no one ever wants hear.

"A human being," Mason responded. "Knowing that is enough."

He walked away, moving across the yard and then the pavement, walking up the church steps. He sat there, back to the spray-painted door.

She could have left him alone.

She probably should have. She thought it was what he wanted, but Chance was talking to the sheriff and Cyrus was speaking with a deputy, and Trinity was alone, looking at a man who seemed lonelier than anyone should ever be.

She walked slowly, telling herself with every step that Mason would tell her to go away before she ever reached his side.

Telling herself that his loneliness was none of her business, that his sadness was nothing to do with her.

He's a human being, he'd said, and the words had been filled with a depth of compassion and heartache that had made her throat tight and her breath catch.

She made it to the church steps.

They were as old and neglected as the building, the cement cracked and weathered, the wrought-iron railings pulling away from their moorings.

She stood there for a moment, the chaos of the rescue

crews and police investigation behind her, Mason's stillness a complete contrast to it.

He was looking right at her.

She knew that.

Despite the darkness and the rain and the chaos, she knew it. He didn't tell her to go away. He didn't ask what she wanted. She started up the stairs, her heart thumping painfully, her mind filled with words she wanted to say, her heart filled with Mason's silence.

She didn't know him.

She didn't really need to.

She understood what she was seeing—the hurt of a past was sometimes too much to bear.

She reached the top of the stairs and he scooted over, leaving enough room for Trinity to sit. The cement was coated with ice and water, and it seeped through her sweatpants, but she stayed where she was, looking at the world from Mason's perspective—the lights that shone near the road, the flashing emergency lights, the shadowy figures moving through the scene. The man, still and lifeless, surrounded by people who desperately wanted to help him.

She shivered. Not from the cold but from the stark reality of what could be lost. No matter who the young man was, no matter what he'd done, if he died, there would be no second chances.

"You're cold," Mason said, his voice gruff and hard.

"No. I'm sorry," she responded, touching his hand.

He wrapped his fingers around hers, tugging her to her feet. "Do you even know what you're sorry for?" he asked.

"If you tell me, I will."

"Maybe another time, Trinity. When we're not standing out in the freezing rain watching a young man lose his life."

"He may live."

"Let's hope he does. Everyone needs a second chance."

"I was thinking about that."

"Second chances?"

"My sister didn't have one."

"I thought you had two brothers."

"And an older sister. She was kidnapped while she was on a mission trip in South America."

She normally didn't talk about her sister, but Mason seemed to need the distraction and she was willing to provide it.

"I'm sorry. That must have been tough for your family."

"It was. My sister was almost twenty years older than me, so I only have a few really good memories of her, but she left a hole in the family. It's one we all try to fill in our individual ways."

"Is that why your brothers started their company?"

"HEART isn't a company. It's a mission, and my brothers are very dedicated to it."

"A mission?" He led her down the stairs and, when they reached the bottom, he didn't release her hand.

She didn't pull away, either.

She could have.

Easily.

His grip was light, his palm warm against her chilled skin. She told herself that's why she held on—for the warmth. "A mission to reunite families. To find the missing. To bring them back to the people who love them."

"That's a heavy burden."

"Not for them."

"You say that as if you're not part of it."

"I work for the organization, but I'm more office help than team member."

"That's not what I heard," he said, stopping at the edge

of the parking lot, the emergency lights flashing across his face.

"What did you hear?"

"That you could find anything or anyone."

"Who told you that?"

"Your brother and Agent Michaels."

"They're both exaggerating."

"They also said you're a computer forensic expert."

"I'm good at following cyber trails, if that's what you mean."

"I do." He watched her intently, his eyes dark in a hard and handsome face. He wasn't the kind of guy she'd ever been attracted to. She preferred guys who didn't look like they could scare a criminal into confessing.

But there was something very appealing about Mason.

"Okay, then. Yeah. I'm good at it."

"You can get in back doors of computer systems."

"Most systems. Is there a point to this?"

"I don't usually engage in idle conversations, Trinity."

"I'll take that as a yes. So how about you tell me what the point is. It's been a long day. I'm tired and I'm in no mood to answer a bunch of questions."

"I'll cut to the chase, then. I want you to try to hack into my computer mainframe."

"What? Why?" she whispered, looking around as if they were having an illicit conversation about illegal things.

"Because I think the guys who were at my house tonight were trying to get their hands on my computer system. I have files that they might want."

"Okay." She wasn't sure where the conversation was heading but she was willing to go there with him.

"If I'm right, this might not have been their first attempt to access the files. They might have tried to access the files remotely. I'm assuming it's possible to retrace cyber trails, find hackers at their source."

"Of course."

"Have you done it before?"

She had. A few times. She'd worked for the state police, for a local mortgage lender and a private investigator who'd been certain someone had been accessing his secure files. "Yes, but it's not my area of expertise. I'm more of a trail tracker."

"Would it be your area of expertise if I agreed to talk to your friend and her son?"

"What?" she asked, not sure she'd heard him right.

"You see what you can find out about my computer system and files, and I'll talk to your friend and her son. If I decide not to help them, I'll send them to someone just as good."

"There is no one as good as you."

"There are many, many good people who do what I do. Several of them work exclusively with children."

She didn't know if she could help him. She had no idea if she could find any evidence of system infiltration on his hard drive. Even if she did, there was no guarantee she could trace it to its source.

She must have spent too long thinking about it because he leaned down so that they were eye to eye. "I really need your help, Trinity. I could ask Agent Michaels, but that will mean giving up my computer system, and I'm not doing that without a fight."

"What's on there that you're so protective of?"

"Information about clients."

"It must be pretty inflammatory information." And, she wasn't sure she wanted to get involved. Not if it was something the government wanted in on.

"It's not. At all."

"Then why is the government after it?"

"It's a long story, Trinity. And we don't have time to hash it out." He glanced toward the emergency vehicles, frowning as someone stepped from the crowd. She followed his gaze.

Agent Michaels. And he didn't look happy. Thanks to the flashing emergency lights, she could see his frown from across the yard.

"I don't like making rash decisions." Which *totally* explained why she'd left Maryland without telling anyone in her family what she'd planned to do when she reached Maine. Thankfully Mason didn't point that out.

"What would be rash about it? You came to Maine with an agenda. I'm willing to help you achieve your goal. I'll even give you financial compensation if you want."

"I don't." But she did want to help Bryn and Henry.

"Then what do you want?"

"To keep from getting into trouble with the FBI?" she whispered, trying really hard not to look at Agent Michaels. Of course, she did look, and she could see that he was heading straight toward them.

"There is nothing illegal about what you'd be doing. You know that."

True. She did.

"And you'll be helping four people."

"You. Henry. Bryn. Who's the fourth?"

"One of my clients. I'm worried he might be in danger, and I'm concerned that an outside entity might be hacking into my computer to access information about him. Like I said, I could go to someone else, but you're here, and this is a good deal for both of us." He seemed sincere, his dark eyes looking straight into hers, and she wanted to help him almost as much as she wanted to help Bryn.

Just say no! her saner self screamed.

So, of course, she opened her mouth and did exactly the opposite.

"Okay. I'll help."

"Thanks," Mason said, squeezing Trinity's hand and then releasing it. He shouldn't have been holding it, anyway. He'd known that. He'd only meant to help her to her feet, but her skin had been cool and smooth. Her hand had fit so easily in his and he'd told himself that he didn't want her to slip on the icy steps.

And then, somehow, they'd continued to hold hands as they discussed his plan. The one he'd come up with about three minutes before he'd voiced it.

He'd been sitting on the steps, catching his breath, clearing his mind, centering himself in the only way he'd ever been able to—prayer. Because that's what had gotten him through his time in the military, the death of his daughter, the breakup of his marriage.

There were plenty of times when he doubted God's existence. His goodness. His love. But he still turned to Him in prayer when life got hard, when things were rocky, when he had no idea what direction to turn. There was calm in the midst of turmoil when he became still and listened.

And sometimes…

Sometimes he really thought he heard God speak to his heart. Not in audible words. Not in any definable way, but in a quiet assurance that He was there.

So he'd been sitting and praying, and he'd seen Trinity walking toward him. It was as if he'd known her for years. Because he'd known what she'd do. He'd known she'd stop at the bottom of the stairs and he'd known she'd hesitate. He'd known that she'd finally approach him and that she'd sit without speaking.

She'd done all those things and, when he'd helped her to

her feet, he'd known she wouldn't pull away. Even though she could have.

He didn't believe in love at first sight, but there was something about Trinity he didn't think he could resist. Not if they spent much more time together.

That should have been enough to make him keep his distance. It would have been enough if he hadn't been worried about her. She had her brothers. She seemed to have a team of people willing to drop what they were doing to help her out of trouble, but she also seemed to walk into trouble. A lot.

And until the person responsible for the break-in at his house was found and behind bars, there was no guarantee that Trinity wouldn't walk right into more danger. He wanted to keep an eye on her and he wanted her expertise to help him locate the person behind the scenes, the one calling the plays and making decisions. If promising to talk to Trinity's friend and her son gave him both of those things, he was willing to do it.

He would have explained that to her, if she'd asked.

But she seemed too tired for words, all the animation gone from her pale face.

"How are you two doing?" Agent Michaels asked, moving into their close circle before Mason could ask Trinity if she was okay.

"Fine," she said with the same fake-cheerful voice he'd heard her use before.

"Are you sure?" Agent Michaels asked. "I heard you ran into some trouble tonight."

"I've been running into trouble nonstop since I crossed the border into Maine," she responded, running a hand down her wet face. It didn't do any good. The floodgates had opened and rain was pouring from the sky. She could brush the water away all she wanted. It would be back in seconds.

"That's interesting, isn't it?" Agent Michaels smiled, but there was nothing warm or kind in his face.

Trinity must have sensed that. She tensed, her eyes narrowing. "Not really."

"Of course it is. Everything was quiet around here until you showed up."

"Are you implying that I brought the trouble with me?"

"I'm not implying anything. I'm just stating a fact. Sheriff Dillon told me they haven't had a robbery in town in over a year."

"And?"

"Now they've had a break-in, an attempted kidnapping, a murder."

"The young man died?" Mason asked, glancing toward ambulance crew.

"I should have said attempted murder. He's still alive—barely. Either of you two know him?"

"No," Mason and Trinity said in unison.

She met his eyes, offered a tentative smile. "Jinx?"

"This isn't the time for games, Trinity," Agent Michaels said. "Are you sure you don't know the victim?"

"I'm sure."

"And you, Mason?"

"I'm sure."

"Sheriff Dillon knows him." The FBI agent's words came out quickly and Mason tensed. He didn't think he was going to like what he was about to hear.

"He's from town?"

"He's a part-time deputy with Whisper Lake's Sheriff's Department. He was on the scene tonight at your place, helping with the investigation."

Yep. He definitely didn't like what he was hearing.

"There were a lot of people on the scene," Mason responded, his mind playing through all the variables, trying to make sense of the new information. The guy calling the shots had deep pockets. That's what he kept coming back to. Deep enough to pay people to do his dirty work.

"True, but he was there and now he's here. Somehow he arrived before anyone called in a crime."

"He wasn't in uniform," Mason noted.

"I noticed. So what's he doing at an abandoned church?"

"Did he smoke?" Trinity asked.

"I have no idea. Why?"

"The guy who grabbed me smelled like cigarettes and alcohol."

"Then it wouldn't surprise me if the deputy smells like both."

"You think he tried to kidnap me?" Trinity sounded genuinely surprised.

Mason wasn't. People would do a lot of ugly things for very small amounts of money.

"Can you think of another reason why he was out here in the rain, his shoes caked with mud, twigs stuck in his clothes, pine needles in his hair?"

"A bullet in his stomach," Mason added.

Agent Michaels shook his head. "He was shot in the back. The bullet went straight through. Probably did a lot of internal damage."

"Same caliber as the one used at my place?"

"We're still searching for the bullet. Just so you know, Mason, the deputy wasn't just at the scene of the break-in. He was helping process the scene inside your house."

"I need to head home." Mason strode past Agent Michaels, his muscles tight, his stomach churning with helpless fear.

"What's wrong?" Trinity ran up beside him, taking two

strides for every one of his, her face even paler than it had been.

"That computer system I want you to look at is at my house. It contains sensitive material—client information I don't want getting into the wrong hands."

"What would be the wrong hands?" she asked.

He could have ignored the question. He could have told her to find her brother and go back to the inn, but Trinity was in this as deep as anyone and she deserved answers. "I'm not sure, but I think whoever it is wants to stop one of my clients from testifying at a court-martial hearing." He explained quickly as he dodged through a crowd of people watching as the deputy was carried to the ambulance.

Judah was standing a few feet away, his expression grim. He didn't stop watching the gurney until it was on the ambulance. Then he turned to Mason and shook his head.

"I'm sorry. He passed all the background checks. He grew up in town. He's a good kid. Or he always seemed to be."

"You can't blame yourself for this, Judah."

"Sure I can, but blaming anyone isn't going to do any good. Is there anything you two need before I head to the hospital?"

"A ride back to my house and permission to enter it."

"You're afraid he took something?"

"I'm afraid he found a way into my office."

"I hadn't thought that far yet, but it's a legitimate concern. I'll drive you over. They finished processing the scene, so getting you inside shouldn't be a problem. Come on. Let's head out."

Judah stalked across the yard and Mason followed, Trinity jogging along beside him. "Do you think they'll let you in the house?" she asked, and he nodded.

"I think they're going to have to." Because Mason *was* going inside. He didn't care who tried to stop him. If the system had been compromised, Tate needed to be warned.

He needed to be warned, anyway, because there was no telling how many people were hunting him or how high the bounty on his head. And there was one. Mason was certain of it. A good kid from a nice town who'd never committed a crime didn't go rogue for a pittance. If the fallen deputy was involved, then he'd been paid well to be.

Mason had allowed the authorities to collect evidence. He'd stayed out of the way while they'd processed the scene at his house. Now he was going to do his own investigating. He was going to find Tate, warn him, and then he was going to track down the guy calling the shots and he was going to stop him.

NINE

They were five minutes away from the old church when Trinity's phone buzzed. She knew who it was before she glanced at the Caller ID. Chance was looking for her. She should have let him know she was leaving, but she'd been busy trying to keep pace with men who were bent on getting where they were going quickly. She hadn't had time to.

Even if she had, she might not have done it.

The truth was, she didn't have the energy to argue with her brother. Not that he'd have argued about her going to Mason's place. He'd probably have insisted on accompanying her, but she wouldn't have minded that. What they would have argued about was her involvement in the case. Chance wouldn't want her helping with a computer forensic search. Not when it was connected to a volatile situation. He'd want her to get on the next plane to Maryland. She had no intention of doing that. They'd be at cross-purposes and that would lead to an epic battle.

Okay. Not epic. Not even a battle. Chance wasn't that kind of guy. He'd take a more subtle approach, reminding her that their parents were vacationing in Europe and would be brokenhearted if anything happened to her.

As if she needed a reminder. Every time she walked into her parents 1970s ranch house, she was confronted by their loss and their sorrow. Not that they hadn't moved on. They had. But there were pictures of Trinity's sister everywhere. A few of her ratty stuffed animals sitting on doll rocking chairs or bookshelves, photo albums, newspaper articles, even journals that had been shipped back from her mission trip. Trinity had poured over them when she was a kid. Back then, she'd believed she'd find a clue that would restore her family.

It had never happened and eventually she'd stopped looking. For some reason she'd felt like a failure because of that. If she was honest with herself, that failure had shaped her choice of careers. She wanted to follow trails, figure out the significance of the most insignificant thing. By the time she'd entered college, computer forensics had been a thing and she'd jumped on board.

She didn't regret her career choice.

She just wasn't sure it would have been her choice if her sister's disappearance hadn't shaped her journey.

Her phone buzzed again and she sighed, pulling it from her pocket, her elbow jabbing Mason in the ribs.

"Sorry," she mumbled.

He shrugged. "Not your fault. I could have sat up front."

"Why didn't you?"

"You looked like you might pass out, so I didn't want to leave you back here alone."

"That's...sweet?"

"Mercenary," he corrected. "I need your help, remember? If they haul you off to the hospital, I'm not going to get it. Not quickly, anyway."

"I don't need to go the hospital and you aren't the kind of guy who needs anyone's help," she responded, not interested in whatever game he was playing. She was going to help him because she believed he'd follow through and meet with Bryn and Henry, but she didn't think he needed her expertise any more than she needed five more minutes standing in the rain.

"Everyone needs help sometimes," he responded.

Something in his voice made her turn her head, look into his dark eyes. When she did, she was caught in his gaze, surprised by that hint of loneliness, the sadness that was barely hidden.

Not her business.

She'd been down Love Avenue before. She'd walked it hand in hand with one of the nicest guys she'd ever met. Dale had been sweet and funny and charming.

And a cheating, lying, two-timing jerk!

The sad thing was she'd seen the signs. She'd had some suspicions. She just hadn't wanted to believe what her gut was telling her.

She swallowed bitterness that tasted like bile and offered Mason her best fake smile. "You're right. I misspoke. You obviously need my help with your computer system."

"All right," he said quietly. "We'll go with that."

"What's that supposed to mean?"

"Your phone is buzzing," he replied.

He was right.

It was. Buzzing incessantly, the texts coming in fast and furious. She could have continued to ignore them, but Chance never gave up. He was probably already trying to track her phone signal.

She punched his number, waiting while the phone rang twice.

He answered on the third ring, his voice gravely and sharp with anger. "Where are you?"

"On the way to Mason's place."

"Are you nuts? You were nearly kidnapped twice tonight. The safest place for you is on a plane heading home."

"No plane is going to take off in this kind of weather. At

least, not any private plane," she pointed out, sidestepping his comment about heading home. She'd made a deal with Mason. If she followed through, he would, too. Maybe once he met Bryn, once he talked to Henry, he might change his mind and agree to make the prosthetic leg.

"Stop sidestepping the issue," Chance growled. "You walked away from a mission without permission."

"We weren't on a mission—"

"Yeah. We were. It was mission Keep Trinity Alive. And you're not making it easy to be successful."

"I'm with Sheriff Dillon."

"You mean the guy who had the man who kidnapped you on his payroll?"

"He attempted to kidnap me. He wasn't successful."

"You're splitting hairs."

"I'm trying to talk you down from your adrenaline high. I wasn't kidnapped by the deputy, and I'm currently with the sheriff and Mason. I doubt they're in cahoots, luring me off to my doom for some nefarious reason."

"Cahoots?" Mason repeated, his amusement obvious.

"I don't care who you're with, Trinity. Protocol dictates that when we're on a mission, no member of the team deviates from the plan without informing the leader of his intentions."

"I wouldn't know about that. I've never been on a mission."

"You helped with Stella's grandmother," he reminded her. A fellow HEART member, Stella had been attacked while she was caring for her elderly grandmother. It had been a tough situation and one that had required help from several team members. It had also led to Stella and Chance finally doing what they should have done years ago—getting married.

"I babysat her while you and Stella ran off and did the

hard work." Trinity hadn't minded nearly as much as she probably should have. She loved Stella's grandmother. Beatrice had Alzheimer's, but she still remembered her granddaughter, her friends and Trinity. She loved *Little Women*, Christmas and everything to do with family. She and Trinity had bonded during the time they'd spent together, and now they spent a couple of weekends a month together, shopping, getting their nails done and revisiting all the things Beatrice loved but sometimes forgot.

"Every member of the team has a job," Chance said, continuing with the same tired lecture he'd been giving her since he'd hired her. "Yours is no less important—"

"Than anyone else's. You've told me that enough times that I'm not going to forget."

"I've told you that, because what you do for the team is extraordinarily valuable. Without your work—"

"Chance," she cut him off. "We've been over this dozens of times. There's no need to revisit it."

"Obviously there is. Stella said you've been dissatisfied at work. She's been implying that you'd like a bigger role in the organization."

"Traitor," she muttered, but she couldn't be angry at Stella. She meant well and she had Trinity's best interest at heart. Plus, she was family. She and Chance had been married for nearly a month. The perfect couple, they were everything Trinity had hoped to be with Dale.

She didn't like the twinge of jealousy she felt when she spent time with the two of them, and she didn't ever allow herself to dwell on it. God had a plan for her life. A good one. One that was perfect for her.

So what if it was taking forever for Him to reveal it?

Eventually, He would.

She hoped. She squeezed the bridge of her nose as Chance continued with the well-worn lecture. She couldn't blame him for giving it. She had broken protocol, and she knew it. It wasn't like she didn't sit in on HEART meetings, hadn't heard Chance issue the same information to every team member.

"Let me," Mason said, taking the phone from her hand. The move was so unexpected she didn't even try to stop him. By the time she'd realized she should have, he was already talking to her brother.

"Chance? It's Mason. Your sister is fine. You can meet us at my place if you're worried." He met her eyes as he listened to Chance's response. "Right. See you then."

He handed her the phone, settled back against the leather seat.

"What'd he say?" she asked.

"Do you really want to know?"

"I really want to get out of these wet clothes. I'm only mildly curious about your conversation with him."

He chuckled, his gaze still on her. "He told me that if anything happened to you, he'd hold me personally responsible. He also said that I'm not to let you out of my sight. And…he's on the way."

"Perfect."

"There's nothing wrong with someone caring, Trinity," the sheriff said. He'd been silent since they'd left the church parking lot, his expression guarded, his shoulders tense. "I have four older brothers and two sisters. There isn't one of them that doesn't like to try to tell me how to live my life. That's not smothering or controlling. It's love. Every time I get annoyed, I remind myself of that."

"Must be interesting to live life with other people always wanting to be involved," Mason said. The emphasis he put on *interesting* made it really clear that he didn't actually think it would be.

"You don't have family?" she asked.

He shook his head. "I'm an only child. Both my folks died when I was young."

"I'm sorry."

"They weren't exactly stellar parents, Trinity. I was being raised by my grandparents before either of them passed away."

"I'm sorry about that, too."

"I'm not. My grandparents were good people. What values I have, they instilled in me." They'd reached the turn-off to Mason's property and he leaned forward, staring through the small window that separated the front and back of the squad vehicle.

Trinity looked, too, but there wasn't anything to see. The road was empty, no cars or lights visible.

"Looks quiet," he said, and the sheriff nodded.

"I think everyone has cleared out. There wasn't a lot to find. Mostly fabric fibers and hair. We collected a few bullets in the woods and a couple of K-9 teams may still be out there. Not likely, though. Not in this kind of weather."

"Good. I don't much like a bunch of strangers congregating on my property."

"I don't much like having crime in my community. So I guess we're even." Judah pulled up to Mason's house, climbed out of the car and opened the door for Trinity. "Your Jeep is still here. It didn't look like there'd been any action near it, so we didn't tow it to the evidence lot."

"That's great." It would have been better if she had her keys. Unfortunately those had been lost at some point during her mad dash through the forest. Maybe they'd been located. If so, she'd have a vehicle to get around in.

"We found keys and a cell phone near the edge of the yard. We'll have to keep both," he added as if he'd read her mind and was answering her unspoken request.

"I understand."

"I'll let you know when we can give them back to you."

"Thanks." She was shivering again, the cold wind bringing more rain and driving it straight through her sopping clothes. She'd left her Jeep unlocked. At least, she'd thought she had. She had clothes there. Sweaters. Extra layers she could bundle up in.

"No problem. I'm heading inside. I want to make sure the evidence team cleaned up before they left."

"You have the spare key I gave you a couple of years ago?" Mason asked. "Or do you need mine?"

"I've got it." The sheriff was walking toward the back door of the house.

"We'd better get inside, too. Before you end up as cold as you were before we went to the hospital." Mason touched her shoulder, and she felt the strange urge to lean into him, to let herself relax for just a few minutes.

Obviously, she was a lot more tired than she'd realized.

But not so tired that she was ready to go inside. She was more interested in going around to the front of the house, because she really needed warm, dry clothes. She also wanted to grab the photo album she'd tucked into her carry-on. There were pictures of Bryn and Henry in it. She'd included photos of Bryn's husband, of the tiny house they'd lived in before he was killed. She and Henry still lived there. Right around the corner from Trinity, because Trinity had wanted to be close enough to walk over during the middle of the night when Bryn was lonely and crying for the love of her life.

"Trinity?" Mason's hand shifted from her shoulder to her cheek, and her breath caught, everything inside of her stilling.

He was closer than she'd realized—just inches away, his clothes as wet as hers, his flannel shirt clinging to a broad chest and muscular biceps.

And if she let herself she could see him as something he wasn't—some kind of hero running to her rescue, the answer to some unspoken prayer, some unfulfilled desire. Eventually, she'd realize he wasn't any of those things. She'd be disappointed the way she had been with Dale.

She didn't want that any more than she wanted to disappoint Bryn.

"I want to grab some things from my Jeep. It will only take a minute."

"Let's go, then." He hooked his arm through hers and started walking, his body warm even through layers of wet, cold clothes. And it was there again, the urge to lean closer, to absorb a little of his heat, let it settle into her and chase away the chill.

But, of course, she couldn't.

He was nearly a stranger, and she hadn't ever even leaned on Dale. They hadn't had that kind of relationship. Which, maybe, had been part of the problem.

They rounded the house side by side and she could feel the tension ease from Mason as they moved deeper into the silence of his property.

"How long have you lived here?" she asked, the question popping out before she could stop it.

They weren't friends and they probably never would be, and it was really none of her business, but she wanted to know more about Mason. She could admit that. Just like she could admit that she liked the feel of his arm against hers, that she was attracted to his quiet confidence.

"You didn't find out during your research?" he responded, stopping at her Jeep.

She tried the door, was relieved to find it open.

"I know how long you've owned the property. I have no idea when you started living here." She climbed in, reaching over the backseat to grab her overnight bag.

It was heavy. She hadn't packed light because she hadn't been sure how long she'd planned to stay. It took time to plan a life. Especially a life that had become a train wreck of bad decisions.

She yanked the bag, but couldn't budge it.

"You could open the hatch," Mason suggested, reaching past her to push the button and open the back.

"I would have, but that would have made things easier and I'm all about doing things the hard way," she replied. It was supposed to be funny. She sounded pitiful instead.

"Pity party, Trinity? You don't really seem like that kind of person." He walked around to the back and grabbed her bag.

"It was a joke."

"Sure," he said.

"It was."

"Is there anything else you need before we go inside?" He changed the subject. Which she should have appreciated because there *had* been a little bit of truth in her words and a little bit of self-pity in her tone. Instead she felt frustrated and annoyed. Usually she was cheerful, happy, an optimist who enjoyed looking at the bright side of things.

Lately she was a Debbie Downer.

She knew it, and she hated it, but she felt helpless to change it.

The big 3-0 coming up in a couple of years, Stella had told her when she'd shared her frustration. *And your life isn't what you'd thought it would be. Of course you feel a little blue. What you need is a hobby. Something that doesn't involve computers or spending time with my grandmother.*

"Trinity?" Mason prodded, the bag still in his hand. "Is there anything else you need?"

"My purse." The photo album was in it. So was her wallet, her key ring with her house keys, her ID.

She opened the center console. She'd left the small bag there. Just like she always did.

Only it was gone.

"It's gone," she said, and Mason stepped closer.

"What's gone?"

"My purse."

"You're sure?"

"As sure as I am that you're standing there." She checked under the front seat. Just to be sure. Climbed into the back as Mason set the bag on the front seat.

"What's it look like?" he said, climbing into the back with her. It wasn't a large Jeep and he was a big guy. They were crowded together, shoulders bumping, feet touching.

"Small. Pink."

"Pink?"

"Is there something wrong with that?" she asked, reaching under the backseat and coming up empty again.

"I didn't take you for a pink kind of woman."

She stopped searching for the purse, looked straight into his gorgeous eyes and told herself that he didn't already know her better than Dale ever had. "What makes you say that?"

"Just a hunch. Doesn't look like we're going to find it I here. You're sure you didn't have it when you walked to my door?" He took her hand, pulling her from the Jeep.

"I'm sure."

"Maybe the police took it in as evidence."

"Why?"

"How about we ask Judah?" He grabbed her bag and turned toward the house. "He's probably already made himself comfortable. We might as well stir things up a little."

"They haven't been stirred up enough for one night?" she asked, distracted by the thought of her purse in the hands an unknown entity. If the police or the FBI had it, that was fine, but if the guys who'd chased her through the woods did…

She shuddered and Mason dropped an arm around her shoulder, tugging her close his side.

She should have been surprised but she wasn't.

She also should have been appalled.

But, of course, she wasn't that, either. There was nothing romantic about the gesture, nothing forward. He was providing warmth that she obviously needed, and she was taking it because she was half frozen again.

Simple.

A courteous gesture. Nothing more. But it felt better than anything had in a long time. It felt more natural than taking her next breath, and that terrified her.

"You should have kept Agent Michaels's coat," Mason said as he led her to the front door. He fished a key from his pocket, his arm dropping from her shoulder, and it would have been like it had never been there. Except that she could still feel his warmth.

"I don't like to owe people."

"And yet, you don't mind being owed."

"Another thing you've guessed about me?" she asked as he unlocked the door and led her into a small foyer. A wide doorway on the left opened into a living room. To the right, another door opened into a well-outfitted office.

"Is this the computer you want me to look at?" she asked, standing in the doorway and eyeing the system.

"No." He set her bag down and stepped into the room, walking across gleaming wood floors to a wall lined with bookshelves. He pressed his fingers to a spot beneath one of the shelves and the entire wall slid sideways—bookshelves and all.

Behind it was another smaller room.

Not much there. Just a computer monitor and hard drive, a chair, a file cabinet and photos. They were everywhere—pictures of men and women in uniform and in civilian clothes.

"Your secret bat cave?" she murmured, moving into the space.

"If I were a superhero, maybe," he responded.

She just nodded, her attention caught and held by one picture after another. A few were of hospital rooms and patients lying in beds, limbs wrapped, faces pale, eyes hollow. Even their smiles couldn't hide the trauma they'd lived through.

"My clients," he said as he walked in behind her. He flicked a light switch on a wall and the computer monitor came to life. "I like to remind myself."

"Of the good work you're doing?"

"Of the reason why I do it." He said it quietly, that hint of sorrow and loneliness in his voice. She heard it the same way she'd seen it in his eyes.

"Mason?" Sheriff Dillon called. "You in here?"

"Yeah. Come on back."

"Anything missing?" the sheriff asked as he walked into the room.

"They weren't able to access it."

"You're sure?"

"Only my fingerprints can open it. They'd have had to chop through the shelving wall to get in, so I'd know if they'd been here."

"That's something, then."

"Sheriff Dillon," Trinity began, and he held up a hand.

"How about just calling me Judah? That's what I go by. Even when I'm on duty."

"Okay." She agreed because she didn't care what she called him. She wanted answers to a few questions. "Was my car searched while the evidence team was here?"

"There was no need. There wasn't any evidence that the perps had been on this side of the house."

"Someone was in it," she said. "My purse is missing."

"You're sure?" He asked the same question Mason had.

"She's sure," Mason replied. "We searched the vehicle and it's not there."

"Is it possible you dropped it when you exited the vehicle?"

"No."

"Tell you what… I'll make a few calls. See if maybe I'm wrong about the vehicle being searched."

"I hope you are. My wallet was in the purse. My house keys."

The two men exchanged glances and she knew what they were thinking—anyone who wanted access to her house and her life could easily get it. Address on her driver's license. Key in her purse. They had everything they needed to take anything they wanted.

"I should probably call my bank and cancel my bank cards," she said, pulling out her cell phone.

"That's a good idea," Mason said. "Judah, how about we take a look around her Jeep? Maybe we'll see something I didn't notice when I was out there before."

The two men walked out of the room and Trinity had no doubt they were planning to discuss her while they were gone. She didn't care. All she wanted was what had been taken. She didn't care about the money in her account. It didn't matter if a thief took every cent of the money she'd been saving for her wedding and honeymoon. She was worried about her apartment in Annapolis and about Marjorie Mae. Her landlady watered the plants when Trinity was away and if she walked in on someone riffling through Trinity's things, the elderly woman could be hurt. Or worse.

Forget the bank. She was calling Jackson. He lived close enough to drive to her apartment and check things out. He could also find someone to install a new lock. The ninety-year-old could do a lot of things, but maintenance work on the apartment wasn't one of them.

So that was the plan. Call Jackson. Have him visit the apartment and install a new lock. After that, she'd call the bank and cancel her cards.

It wasn't a perfect solution to the problem, but it was something and it was better than sitting around hoping for the best.

Satisfied, she dialed Jackson's number and waited for him to answer.

Mason didn't like the way any of this was going down. Sure, it would be nice to believe the purse had been taken as evidence, but he didn't believe that. Not at all.

Someone had searched her Jeep. That same person had taken the purse. More than likely, he was already halfway to Maryland, ready to break into Trinity's apartment and wait for her there.

Or find something he could use to manipulate her into a situation he could use to his advantage.

He frowned, moving across the yard with Judah beside him. They'd known each other for enough years that conversation flowed easily, but neither of them was speaking. Knowing Judah, he was deep in his own thoughts, trying to piece together the very disparate pieces of a very complicated puzzle.

They reached the Jeep and worked side by side, moving around the vehicle with slow deliberation, crouching next to areas that might have been tamped down by boots or sneakers. It was obvious people had been around, but it was impossible to tell if any of them had been in the Jeep.

"We're not going to find anything," Judah finally said. "We might as well go back in."

"Giving up a little easily, aren't you?"

"You have another suggestion?"

"Yeah. Check your deputy's squad car and house." It was just an idea, formed and spoken almost before Mason had processed it.

"Which one?"

"The one in the hospital."

"Chad Williams. That's his name. His parents are going to be devastated if he dies. They're going to be more devastated when they find out he tried to kidnap a woman." He ran a hand down his jaw, obviously upset and angry. "I hope I don't have to add stealing to that list."

"If their son dies, it might be best to keep the rest quiet."

"Might be best, but probably won't be possible. This is a small town. People talk. Even my deputies are prone to gossip. Wouldn't surprise me if the news has already started spreading."

"I'm sorry."

"Yeah. Me, too. But you're right. If someone took the purse, he's at the top of the list of suspects. He could have easily opened the door and searched the vehicle, and no one would have said a word."

"That's what I was thinking."

"This situation stinks," Judah conceded. "I'm not going to lie. I didn't sign up for small-town police work because I wanted what I had in New Jersey."

"You worked in New Jersey?" Mason asked, surprised because Judah had never mentioned it before.

But, then, they were more the kind of friends who hiked, fished and hunted together. The whole male-bonding thing wasn't for either of them.

"I was a beat cop. I got tired of arresting smart people for doing stupid things, tired of cleaning up messes other people made, so..." His voice trailed off and Mason assumed he'd felt like he'd said too much.

"So you came to a place where people never did stupid things and where there were never any messes to clean up?" He finished the sentence, and Judah smiled.

"Right. As if there *is* such a place. I came home because it felt like the right thing to do, but it's a lot harder than I imagined it would be to lock up people I've known for most of my life. This? It's even worse because the suspect is a guy I liked and respected." He sighed. "I'm going to head back to the station. I'll look in Chad's squad car and I'll ask his parents' permission to enter his apartment. It's above their garage, so if they give it to me, I won't have to get a search warrant. I'll call you if I locate the purse. Call me if you have any trouble." He stalked away, shoulders hunched against the wind, face down.

Mason watched him go and then climbed into the Jeep. Trinity had left the console open. It was empty except for a packet of peanut butter crackers and a chocolate bar.

Nothing under any of the seats. The glove compartment contained the driver's manual and a twenty-dollar bill. Obviously whoever had taken the purse hadn't taken it for the money. He checked the backseat again, catching a faint whiff of some flowery perfume.

Icy rain splattered on the roof and pinged off the windshield. The sky—still thick with clouds—hung low, the moon hidden.

He loved this part of the world.

He loved his parcel of land, his house, his job.

He had no desire to change things up, but there were times when he sat on the porch late at night, listening to the forest noises and wondering what it would be like to have someone beside him.

He frowned, not sure why his thoughts had gone in that direction. Or maybe he was.

Trinity.

She'd exploded onto the scene, bringing all kinds of chaos with her.

Chaos. The thing he always avoided. He wanted calmness, peace and routine. He needed those things. They kept him grounded and kept the monsters at bay.

No way would he ever be attracted to a woman who turned calm into chaos, who brought people and noise and uncertainty.

That wasn't his deal, wasn't his kind of thing.

But he was attracted to Trinity.

He couldn't deny it any more than he could deny the truth about himself. He was a loner. He didn't need people and letting any woman think he did would be a mistake.

He exited the Jeep, closing the door and scanning the darkness as he walked back to the house. The foyer light was on, the soft glow as reassuring as the sound of humming coming from his office.

Humming?

He followed the sound, knowing exactly where it would lead him.

Trinity was still in the secret room, only now she was hunched over his computer, typing frantically.

He didn't want to disturb her and he backed away.

"No need to leave," she said, not even glancing his way.

"Looks like you're working."

"I am."

"On?"

"Just taking a look at your security settings. They seem pretty tight."

"They can't be that tight. I've got a password that should have kept you from getting into the system," he responded, stepping into the room and standing near her arm.

She was still typing and still not looking at him, her fingers flying over the keyboard.

"It was a good password. Not your birthday or your name. Not your address, either. I tried them all."

"It's randomized."

"That's the way it should be. It makes it nearly impossible for anyone to guess it."

"And yet you managed."

"I didn't figure out the password. I came in through a back door. Most systems have them, but most people have no idea how to find them."

"I repeat—you managed it."

"I'm trained to manage it. Of course, once I'm in the system, I've still got to access encrypted files. Did you have a computer programmer set this up for you?"

"Programmer and security expert."

"You must have been very worried about someone getting into these files."

"Client confidentiality is important, and the microchips I build into the prosthetics allow any of my clients to be located at any time."

"Do they know that?" She finally looked at him, her sharp gaze at odds with her summer-blue eyes and her soft lips.

"Of course."

"Who's the guy you're worried about? The one who's witness in a court-martial case?"

"Tate Whitman," he responded.

"You're worried someone is trying to find him and they want to hack your system to do that, right?"

"Yes." He confirmed what he'd told her before and she turned back to the computer, short nails clicking against the keys.

He waited, the minutes ticking by, her focus so complete that she didn't seem to notice when the doorbell rang. He knew her brother and Cyrus had arrived, but he didn't want to leave the room. Not even to answer the door. There was something fascinating about watching her work, something compelling about the complete focus she had.

It reminded him of the way he felt when he worked on a prosthetic and was studying computer data, working out the variables and the measurements.

The doorbell rang again and he finally pulled himself away. He shouldn't be fascinated. He knew that. He shouldn't feel compelled. All he should be doing was trying to find the quickest way to solve his problems and to get Trinity and her chaos out of his house.

That is what he should be doing.

What he *would* be doing. After he figured out how deep into his files Trinity could get, how much she could learn from them and whether or not she was able to find evidence that a hacker had been there before her.

TEN

Three days in Maine was about what Trinity had expected to spend. She just hadn't expected to spend most of that time in a little office in Mason Gains's house. That's exactly what she'd done. Hour after hour hunched over his computer, trying to follow the trail of someone who had most definitely been trying to access his computer files.

They hadn't been successful.

They'd accessed a few of the files that weren't encrypted, but hadn't been able to break the code to access the others. She'd barely managed. It had taken her two twelve-hour days to do it.

"How's it going?" Chance walked into the room, the scent of coffee and doughnuts following him.

"About the same as it was the last time you checked on me. Five minutes ago."

"Five hours ago," he corrected.

She finally looked away from the screen. "Really?"

"Yeah. Really." He set a tray on a small table Mason had brought in. She wasn't sure when. One minute it hadn't been there. The next it had.

"Time flies when you're following trails."

"How about you take a break? Go outside, get a little air?

The weather has cleared. The foliage is beautiful. That is why you came up here, right?"

"Yes."

"So, go enjoy it."

"I'd rather finish what I started." She turned back to the computer, ignoring the coffee and doughnuts and him. She wanted to find the systems operator on the other end of the trail. The sooner she did, the sooner she could leave.

And she needed to leave, because Mason was proving to be a problem.

She frowned, typing more quickly, accessing another system and another. Hitting another wall and backtracking.

"Trinity," Chance said, a world of patience in his voice. Which meant he wasn't feeling at all patient. "You need to get some air."

"I have air."

"You've been sitting there so long, you've probably grown roots."

"I'm sure we'll manage to uproot them when it's time to leave."

"Here's the thing," he said. "It's time. I've got to get home. So does Cyrus."

"So, go."

"We're not going without you."

"Chance." She stopped typing but she didn't look at him. She didn't want to see the concern in his eyes or the worry in his face. "I'm an adult. I have been for a long time. I drove up here by myself and I can manage to drive myself back."

"When you drove up here, you didn't have a price on your head."

"I still don't."

"You can't be sure of that."

"And you can't spend the rest of your life trying to

protect me." She swiveled in the chair, turning it around so she was finally facing Chance. "You have a wife now. You have a home. You have Gertrude and a bunch of other people who count on you."

"And I have you and I'm not going to lose you. I'll give you until tomorrow morning and then we need to leave. The plane will be ready at dawn." He walked out of the room and left her there, his words echoing in the sudden silence.

She wanted to leave, so his ultimatum shouldn't have bothered her. It didn't bother her. Not really. She needed to return to Maryland. She had an apartment there, friends, a job.

And it wasn't like she couldn't continue the hunt there. She'd learned Mason's computer system inside and out. She'd followed the trail three times to three different servers, none of which had given her the information she wanted.

She could use the system at HEART, do her tracking from there, and still provide support for the team.

But until she accomplished her goal, she couldn't ask Mason to fulfill his end of the bargain. Henry's surgery was in a week and she wanted to give him a little hope, give Bryn a little reassurance.

She typed more quickly, breaking down firewalls and sneaking into systems, following the trail that had been left and then hitting the same wall she kept finding herself up against. For the first time since she'd begun working in the field, she couldn't break through. Every time she tried, she was booted right back to the beginning.

She tried a different access point and was shut down again, tossed back to the beginning of the trail and the very first system she'd hacked.

Frustrated, she slammed her hand on the table, shoved away from it and nearly upended the tray Chance had left. Coffee slopped from an over-full cup, soaking a powdered-sugar doughnut.

"This is not going to beat me," she muttered.

"Trouble?" Mason asked, his voice so surprising, she nearly toppled from her chair.

She managed to right herself. Barely. And stood wobbling on legs that had spent way too much of the past few hours sitting.

"What are you doing here?" she asked, her heart leaping as she looked into his eyes. This was why she really did need to leave. Three days looking into those beautiful, dark eyes. Three days watching him interact with her brother and Cyrus. Three days realizing that Mason wasn't just a recluse who made prosthetic limbs. He was a really nice guy with a great sense of humor and a deep loyalty to the men and women he'd helped.

She liked that about him.

She liked him.

And that could be a problem.

It *was* a problem. When she'd broken up with Dale, she'd told herself that being single was what she wanted. She didn't need to cater to a man. She didn't need to work hard to make someone else look good.

Fact—I don't need anyone but God, my family and my friends.

She'd scrawled those words in her journal the day after she'd said goodbye to the man she'd pinned way too many dreams on.

"I'm checking on you," he said, taking her hand and pulling her away from the computer. "It's getting late. You haven't eaten all day. How about we go outside? Get some fresh air and sunshine before the day ends and our chance for it is over?"

"Did Chance talk you into saying that?"

"He's worried, and Cyrus was on the phone with his wife. I was the only one available, so, yeah. He did."

"I'm surprised," she said as he led her from the room.

"By what?"

"The fact that you're so easy to manipulate."

"I'm only easy to manipulate when I'm being manipulated into something that I want."

"You want to go outside?"

"I want to get you away from that computer. You've been hunched over it for three days."

"There's nothing unusual about that, Mason. It's what I do for a living."

"Do you spend fifteen hours a day at your job?" he asked.

"Not usually."

"Then you don't need to do it here."

"Yes, I do. I want to give you what you asked for, so I can get what you promised."

"Is that what all your mad typing is about? What all the skipped meals and late nights have been for—to get me to come through on my part of the bargain?" They'd reached the foyer and he opened a closet, pulling out a soft, flannel jacket.

"There's more to it than that."

"Like?" He helped her into the jacket, zipping it up to her chin and then pulling her hair out of her collar. His hand brushed her jaw, her neck, the tender skin behind her ears.

"This is the only thing I'm good at, Mason. I'm not willing to fail at it."

He laughed, the sound ringing through the hallway.

"It's not funny."

"Yeah. It is." He opened the door and they walked outside. The day was as beautiful as her brother had said, the trees red and yellow and orange.

"Wow," she breathed, reaching for Mason without thinking about it, clutching his arm as they walked down the stairs.

"It's beautiful," she said, and he stopped, touched her chin so that she had to look into his eyes. He wasn't laughing. Not anymore.

"You didn't ask me why what you said was funny." They were a yard from the house, a dozen yards from the woods. There was beauty all around her, vibrant colors, beautiful foliage, but all she could see was him.

"Maybe I didn't want to know."

"You are an innately curious person, Trinity. Of course you want to know."

He was right. Again.

"How do you do that?" she asked, releasing his arm and walking toward the woods, searching for the path that led to the lake.

"Do what?"

"Read me so well."

"You're easy to read."

"Not according to my ex." The words were out before she could stop them and she pressed her lips together to keep more from escaping.

"You've been married?"

"Engaged."

"When did you dump him?"

"How do you know I did the dumping?"

"Because no guy in his right mind would dump you."

"I'm sure there are plenty who would."

"Not a point I'm going to argue," he responded. "So, how long has it been?"

"A few months."

"What did he do? It had to be something big. Lies? Affairs?"

"Nothing I want to talk about." She ducked beneath the low-hanging branch of an oak and stepped into the woods.

"So, both. The guy must have been a royal jerk."

"Did you not hear me say I didn't want to talk about it?"

"I heard. I'm just trying to understand why it's off the table for discussion."

"Because it's not an easy subject and it's difficult for someone who hasn't been there to understand."

"You're assuming I haven't been there."

"Have you?"

"Yeah. Only I was the jerk and she married me anyway."

His confession surprised her and she stopped, the trees pressing in around them, the afternoon filled with the sounds of birds and animals moving through the foliage. "I didn't see anything about your marriage in the research I did."

"You can't learn everything from computers and newspaper articles."

"You forgot televised interviews," she said in a prissy voice that made her cringe.

He grinned and she found herself smiling in return.

"Well, you did."

"You're right. I forgot that I was interviewed a couple of times. I was married before I entered the military and, by the time I was interviewed, it was over."

"I shouldn't ask you what happened," she said because she really *really* wanted to.

"But you want to?"

"Something like that."

"Felicia and I were too young and too different. We got married because I was joining the military and we thought love was the easy kind of stuff you see in the movies. By the time we realized it wasn't, we were already growing apart. Stuff happened. We were both struggling. I wasn't there for her when she needed me." He shrugged. "Eventually she found someone else and walked out."

"That must have been hard."

"It was one of the easiest things I've ever been through."

"Then I guess you've been through some tough times." She ducked under a tree and kept heading in the direction she hoped would lead to the path.

The conversation had gotten really intimate really fast and she wasn't sure what to make of that. She was comfortable with Mason. That was one of the things she liked about him. There was never any need to be someone she wasn't when she was around him. He'd seen her soaking wet, covered in blood, shivering in the cold. Last night, he'd met her in the hallway when she'd left his office to get a snack. She'd known her hair was a wild mess of tangled curls and her eyes dark with fatigue and red from staring the computer for so long, but he'd walked into the kitchen with her and he'd sat and talked while she'd made a pot of coffee and raided his cupboards. She hadn't thought once about smoothing her hair, changing into something more stylish than old sweats, or putting on makeup to cover the scabbed-over scratches on her cheeks.

"So have you," he said, walking behind her, his feet nearly silent on the fallen leaves. "Out of curiosity," he continued before she could respond, "where are we headed?"

"The path to the lake. I imagine the view is stunning from there."

"It is, but the path is this way." He cupped her shoulders and turned her a hundred and eighty degrees.

"Are you sure?"

"I'm fairly confident," he said dryly, and she blushed, pushing through thick foliage and making her way in the direction he'd indicated.

Five minutes later she stepped out onto the path. She had a fifty-fifty shot at turning the correct direction. She turned left.

"Other way," Mason said, and she sighed, turning in the opposite direction and walking down the steeply sloping path until it opened onto the beach.

The lake was breathtaking, the water still and calm, the bright fall foliage reflected on its surface.

"It's beautiful," she said.

"I've got a little fishing boat tied behind those bushes there. I'll take you out on the water, if you want." He gestured to some bushes clustered close to the water's edge."

"That would be great, but I need to get back to work and, if you take me out on the water, that may not ever happen," she responded, walking to the edge of the water and sitting on the cold, pebbly sand. She didn't care that water was seeping through her jeans or that her tennis shoes were soaked. If she'd had a year to sit and gaze at the water, look at the trees, listen to the world, maybe she could figure out where she belonged and what she was supposed to be doing.

"You still haven't asked me," Mason said, dropping down beside her.

"What?"

"Why your comment was funny."

"You're like dog with a bone."

"And?"

"Go ahead and tell me why it was funny."

"Because," he responded, shifting so that he could look

into her face. "You're good at life, and that's a lot better that being gifted at a skill."

"Good at life?" She laughed but he didn't crack a smile.

"At the things in life that matter—relationships, service, compassion. Those are great skills and important gifts. The world would be a darker place without people like you in it."

She wanted to make light of the comment, pretend it hadn't touched that secret place in her heart where all her dreams were tucked away. But she was looking into Mason's eyes, seeing his sincerity, knowing a compliment like that was the greatest one he could give to anyone.

"That is probably the nicest thing anyone has ever said about me," she said, and he touched her face, his fingers skimming lightly along her cheek. His skin was warm and a little rough, and when he tucked a strand of hair behind her ear, she wanted to turn her head, press her lips to his palm.

"Then you don't spend enough time around the right people," he murmured. He leaned in and, for a split second, she thought he was going to kiss her. For a split second, she wanted him to.

Then the day changed, the forest going silent, the animals gone. The sun was still shining, the leaves were still bright and beautiful, but the air felt…different.

Mason noticed it, too. He scanned the lake then the trees behind them. "I don't like the feel of things. You have your phone?"

"Yes." She fished it out of her pocket.

"Text your brother. Tell him to meet us down here—and to come armed."

She texted quickly, her fingers shaking with adrenaline and fear.

Chance texted back immediately and she tucked the

phone away again. "He and Cyrus are on the way. He said to stay where we are."

"Where we are makes us sitting ducks." He stood, pulling her to her feet. "They want you, Trinity. I've got no doubt about that. They think they can use you as a pawn to get what they want from me."

"You're assuming someone is here. It's possible—"

The crack of gunfire split the air and she was on the ground, Mason covering her, her body pressed into the damp sand. She thought she heard an engine, but she couldn't hear much past the blood pulsing in her ears.

"Listen to me," Mason said, his mouth close to her ear. "They're coming down on mopeds. That's going to make it nearly impossible for them to get a clean shot. We've got to make it to the canoe and we've got to make it there quickly. You ready to run?"

She nodded because she couldn't get enough air in her lungs to speak. And then he was up, yanking her to her feet again, sprinting across the beach, the sound of pursuit growing louder behind them.

They had Trinity's wallet. They knew who she was. They knew what she did for a living, and they had even more reason for wanting her. Her expertise made Mason expendable. It was a shame he hadn't thought of that before he'd decided to take a stroll down to the beach.

He pulled his knife from its ankle sheath, slashing the rope that held his boat to the spindly bushes that grew near the water's edge.

"Get in," he yelled, holding Trinity's arm as she hopped into the aluminum hull. He followed quickly, shoving away from the shore, moving them out into deeper water as quickly as he could. As soon as he was clear, he prepped the outboard motor, his eyes on the woods. He could see movement, knew that the gunman had almost made the beach. They weren't out of range of a gunshot yet. Not even close.

He pulled his Ruger from the holster. "Stay low," he growled, handing it to Trinity. "Shoot if you need to."

He yanked the chord on the motor, praying it would catch quickly. Praying he didn't flood the engine. It was an old boat. One of the few things he had of his grandfather's. It had been patched and repaired and used so much that every year he had to make sure it was water-worthy.

"Please," he prayed, yanking on the chord a third time as two motorbikes sped out of the trees.

The water near the hull exploded, the bullet just missing its mark. Trinity fired back and one of the bikes crashed, the rider scrambling up and diving for cover.

Mason yanked the chord again and this time the engine roared to life, cold water spraying up into his face as he turned the throttle and tried to get them out of rifle range.

Trinity fired again. Then again. Her head peeking up over the side of the boat as she aimed and then took her shot. She was more accurate than most people would be. A second bike fell sideways, the driver tumbling off.

The third made it to the water, his body silhouetted by the sunlight. There was something about his stance that screamed military—straight shoulders, solid stance. He had a long-range weapon. A rifle of some sort.

"Get down, Mason!" Trinity shouted.

He opened the throttle instead, more water spraying up as the boat bounced along the surface, traveling at a speed that might just keep them from dying.

He heard the crack of a rifle, felt the impact as a bullet hit the side of the boat and went straight through, grazing his calf before falling into the bottom of the boat.

"Did he hit you?" Trinity asked, abandoning her post

and crawling toward him, the boat bouncing so much she could barely maintain her balance.

"I'm not worried about me," he responded as water bubbled into the hull. "I'm worried about the boat."

They were taking on water at an alarming rate, the far shore at least three miles away. They might make it halfway there before the boat went down, but halfway wasn't going to do them much good in water this cold.

"Do you have life vests?" she asked handing him the Ruger.

"Under the bench seat. There are two or three."

She grabbed them, handing him one and tugging the other over her head, her gaze on the shore and the man still standing there. "We must be out of range. He's not shooting."

"Maybe he's just waiting for us to sink."

"To what purpose? He needs access to your computer system. Killing you isn't a good way to get it." She took off one of her shoes and pulled off her sock. She used it to plug the hole. It slowed the incoming water, but probably not enough to make a difference.

"Is there anything on board we can bail with?" she asked.

"There's a tackle box in the stern. I've probably got some old bait containers in there."

She nodded, her gaze dropping to his calf. Blood was seeping through the fabric of his jeans, but she didn't comment on it. She crawled through an inch of water, opened the tackle box and pulled out two plastic containers.

"These'll do," she said, calm and cool and completely focused. She handed him one and she used the other, scooping the water at a frantic pace.

He could have told her that it was coming in faster than

she'd ever be able to toss it out, but their only other option was to sit in the boat, waiting to be rescued or to sink.

He slowed the boat, tucked his Ruger into its holster, his gaze still on the beach. All three men were at the water's edge, watching and waiting.

Good. The longer they stayed, the more likely it was that Chance and Cyrus would apprehend them. Mason wanted to have a chat with all three of them, but he especially wanted to talk to the guy who'd fired the rifle. Military. Mason was certain of it, and he had the feeling the guy knew exactly who was calling the shots and paying the bills.

"We're going to sink," Trinity said and, for the first time since the shooting had begun, she sounded scared.

"Not if we bail faster than the water comes in," he responded.

"That," she said through gritted teeth, "is not a possibility. So how about you feed me some other happy platitude?"

"You're a good swimmer?" he offered, and she scowled.

"This is no time to joke."

"You are, and I'm not. If the water wasn't so cold, a sinking boat wouldn't be a problem for either of us."

But the water was cold and it had already soaked through most of Trinity's clothes. He pulled her up onto the bench.

"Stay as dry as you can for as long as you can," he said.

Her scowl deepened. "Thanks for the advice, Mason. I'll keep it in mind."

"Sarcasm suits you," he responded more to keep her irritated than anything. Irritated was better than afraid.

"It's one of my better qualities," she responded, still scooping the water, her hands blue from cold.

"Good to know," he said, his focus on the shore, on the

men who were now running back toward their mopeds. Only one was able to get his started. He took off, skirting the shore and avoiding the woods. The two other men ran, following him in what seemed like a desperate attempt to catch up.

"My brother must be coming," Trinity said, her teeth chattering as she dropped the plastic container and began splashing water over the side of the hull, her movements quick and about as effective as a summer jacket on a winter's day.

They were mid-lake and they were sinking.

That much was clear.

What wasn't clear was how Mason was going to get them out of the situation. Sure, help was on the way, but until there was a boat available, Chance and Cyrus were stuck on shore.

Which meant Mason and Trinity were on their own for a while longer.

Just them, the sinking boat and the God Mason had spent a lifetime praying to but had never really expected anything from.

Maybe it was time to change that.

Maybe today was the day to pray with the kind of faith his grandparents had had. The kind of faith that saved and sustained people no matter life's circumstances.

He needed that now more than he ever had before, because he thought he might survive a half hour in Whisper Lake's frigid waters, but he didn't think Trinity could.

That wasn't something he wanted to think about. It wasn't something he wanted to accept, so he grabbed the plastic tub she'd abandoned and scooped two-handed as he prayed for a rescue he wasn't sure would come in time.

ELEVEN

Trinity had a vivid imagination. As a child she'd spent a lot of time imagining the way she'd die. Morbid, but she'd figured the obsession had come from the loss of her older sister.

In all those imaginings, she'd never once thought about drowning. Ever. She understood water safety. She always swam with friends. She followed all the rules that had been drilled into her head by her overprotective parents and brothers.

Too bad none of them had thought to tell her what to do if she happened to be aboard a boat sinking in frigid water.

Currently she was bailing as if her life depended on it, because it did, and she was telling herself that she wasn't already freezing to death.

She didn't quite believe it.

She was shivering as violently as she had the night she'd tried to escape by swimming to town, and she wasn't even in the water yet.

"I'm closing the throttle," Mason said, his voice the calm in the midst of her storm. "We'll take on less water from waves that way, and maybe buy ourselves a couple more minutes."

"We might need longer than that," she responded, eyeing the shore they were moving toward. Was it getting any closer?

The other shore had certainly gotten farther away. She could see two men moving along the waterline. She assumed they were Chance and Cyrus, but her hands were too cold to check her phone and she didn't have the time to waste doing it.

"Yeah. I know." He eased past her, pulling the tackle box from its spot and grabbing a couple of bobbers from it. "Try to shove one of these in the hole. I thought I might have a patch kit, but it's not here, so we'll have to improvise."

She'd already done that with her sock and it hadn't helped much, but she didn't argue. She took the smallest one and smashed it in with her sock. It didn't stop the water. She didn't even think it slowed it, but doing something felt better than waiting around to die.

She scooped more water as Mason grabbed oars and started paddling. Without the motor running, the waves settled and the water didn't splash over the sides of the boat.

A calm approach is the best approach.

Her father always said that, and Trinity had tried to live by it. Right now, though, she wanted to panic, because all of her scooping and all of Mason's slow paddling weren't keeping the boat from sinking. A couple more minutes and they'd be in the water. No doubt about that.

She had to come up with a plan to survive.

Hypothermia might knock her out and then she'd either drown or freeze. At least, that's what she thought would happen. So she'd stay awake, keep her eyes open, force herself not to give in.

At least she had a life vest on. She wasn't likely to sink.

Rescue crews would be able to find her. That was a plus in the midst of a whole boatload of negatives.

"Are you prepared to swim?" Mason asked quietly, the oars lapping at water that was getting closer and closer to the top of the hull because they were sinking deeper and deeper into the lake.

"Of course," she responded because she was prepared to do whatever it took to survive and because she had no other choice. She certainly wasn't going to float on the surface of the lake waiting to die.

"We're probably a mile and a half out. It's not a bad swim. It's the cold that's going to be a problem."

"I'll be okay," she assured him even though she wasn't sure she would be.

"I figured you'd say that." He set the oars in the bottom of the boat and took both her freezing hands in his. "We stick together, okay? Side by side. Float on your back and kick. That'll be the easiest way to swim with the vest on."

"Okay."

"There's a marina near town and they'll probably be sending rescue boats out from there." He motioned to the left and she could see what looked like small buildings and smaller boats. She thought she saw flashing lights, too, and her heart jumped.

"I think I see a police car heading in that direction."

He squinted then nodded. "You may be right, but they're not going to get here before this boat goes down. We'll be in the water for at least fifteen minutes, and we *are* going to stay together. I don't want to be pulled out of this lake wondering whether or not you've been rescued."

"Trust me," she responded, looking into his beautiful dark eyes, his strong handsome face, "I feel the same."

"It's good to know that we've finally agreed on something." He picked up the oars again, trying to paddle as the boat sank.

Trinity kept scooping water and she kept watching the shore, following the flashing lights as they drew closer to the lake.

Definitely police. Maybe an ambulance.

How long could it possibly take for them to get out on the water to stage a rescue? Fifteen minutes? Twenty? Hopefully not any longer than that because Mason's end of the boat was slipping below the surface of the lake, water pouring in over the top, flooding the vessel. One minute she was sitting on the bench seat, the next she was gasping for breath, her body rigid with shock. She hadn't thought that through, hadn't realized just how quickly the cold would affect her.

She gasped, inhaling a lungful of water and coughing it out, trying to remember the plan.

"It's okay. You're okay," Mason said, his hand wrapping around hers. "They've got a vessel in the water. We'll be out of here before the boat hits the bottom of the lake."

"How deep is the lake?" she asked, her teeth chattering so hard she wasn't sure he'd understand.

"I have no idea," he responded. "So, how about we stick to the plan and head for shore?"

The plan.

Right. Stick together. Float on your back. Kick.

She ran the words through her mind over and over as she tried to coordinate her body and do what she needed to.

"You're okay," Mason said again, and she realized she was gasping, inhaling gulps of air as if she were running rather than floating.

"I know," she responded, finally managing a few kicks. She had no idea what direction shore was, so she went where Mason was leading, and she prayed that wherever they ended up, it was warm and dry and far, far away from any lakes.

She wasn't sure how long they were in the water.

She wasn't sure how close they were to shore. Eventually, though, she got into the rhythm of kicking and floating. Her breathing calmed and the cold felt almost warm.

That probably wasn't a good thing, but at least she wasn't shivering so hard she had no control over her muscles.

"You okay, Trinity?" Mason asked, and she nodded as if he could see the movement.

"Trinity?" he prodded, and she forced herself to speak.

"Great," she said, the one-word answer all she could manage.

"They're almost here."

"Great," she repeated, but she had no idea who they were or even where they were coming to. She wasn't sure if she was really in a lake or if she was home in bed, tucked beneath a warm blanket, dreaming about water and about holding hands with a guy she might have fallen for if she'd met him at a different time.

"Trinity!" someone shouted, and she opened her eyes, looked into Mason's face.

He looked furious.

"What?"

"We stick together, remember?" he growled, his face pale, his lips tinged with blue.

"We are together."

"We're not together if you're off in some dreamworld while I'm swimming to shore," he snapped.

Her sluggish brain realized that he wasn't angry. He was concerned. He was also cold. Really, really cold. She could feel him shivering. That scared a little sense into her and she nodded.

"Okay. Right. Let's go."

She didn't know how it happened, but they were moving again, legs kicking, fingers linked, floating through water that felt like an ice bath.

She thought she heard voices and she tried to raise her head, look around, but she only had the energy to keep moving forward.

"Trinity?" Not Mason. Someone else. She knew the voice but couldn't place it, and she didn't respond, just kept on kicking until something splashed in the water beside her. A life preserver. She grabbed on, still holding Mason's hand as she was tugged to a boat and pulled to safety.

They'd been *that* close to dying.

That being too close for comfort.

Mason wasn't happy about it.

As a matter of fact, he was angrier than he'd been in a long time.

He paced the hospital room he'd been admitted to, a blanket wrapped around his shoulders, his bones still aching from cold. He'd already removed the IV, put on the clothes Chance had brought him and downed three cups of coffee.

Now he was ready to find Trinity.

She'd been worse off than he was, nearly unconscious when they'd pulled her from the water. Ten more minutes. That's what the doctors had told Chance. Ten minutes and Trinity would have been too cold to sustain organ function. Her body would have shut down and she would have died.

The thought filled Mason with pointless rage.

Anger didn't solve problems. Thinking did. And, after thinking things through, he'd decided to find Tate, warn him and see what information he could offer.

First, though, he needed make sure Trinity was okay.

He took another swig of coffee, shuddering as the bitter dregs hit the back of his tongue. The hallway was quiet. The hospital they'd been transported to was three towns away from home, but not as big or as busy as Portland General. They'd almost been transported there, but Mason hadn't liked the idea. The busier the hospital, the easier for someone to hide in it.

He'd asked Judah to bring his car when he came to take Mason and Trinity's statement, because he wasn't hitching a ride home with Chance or Cyrus. They didn't plan to return to his house and he didn't want them to. They were heading to the airport and going home. That's the plan Chance had laid out. They had a secure building in DC where Trinity could stay until the threat against her was neutralized.

That worked for Mason.

He'd visit her after he found the guys who'd nearly killed them. All three men had escaped, but he had a feeling they hadn't gotten far. As a matter of fact, he wouldn't be surprised if they were hanging around the hospital waiting to get another chance at Trinity.

Judah had promised to have a deputy guard her room, but one of his deputies had already sold out. There was no reason to think another one hadn't. The sooner Trinity was able to leave the hospital and go to whatever safe place Chance had planned for her, the happier Mason would be.

He walked to the nurses' station, smiling at the young woman behind the counter. "Can you tell me what room Trinity Miller is in?"

She frowned, glanced at her computer screen and shook her head. "I'm sorry. That's listed as private. We can't give the information to anyone who isn't on our list."

"Who's on your list?"

"Family," she said quickly. "Which does not include boyfriends or significant others."

"I'm just a concerned friend. It's possible I'm on the list."

"Name?" she asked with a put-upon sigh.

"Mason Gains."

She looked up from her computer, her eyes wide. "You're a patient."

"I was. I'm checking myself out."

"Have you consulted with the doctor about that?"

"Not yet."

"It might be a good idea. You and Ms. Miller had severe shocks to your systems. There could be long-term side effects."

"Am I on the list of visitors?" he asked, ignoring her comment.

"Yes," she said. "But I don't think—"

"What room is she in?"

She scowled, wrote something on a piece of paper and handed it to him. Room 410. One floor up.

Mason took the stairs because he was still cold and he wanted to force some blood back into his extremities. When he reached the floor, he followed the room numbers to the end of a long hall and saw a uniformed officer sitting in a chair near a door, reading a book. He patted his pockets, looking for his ID, then realized he'd left it at the house.

Fortunately he knew the red-haired, freckle-faced deputy. Six-foot-four of lean muscle, Sam Torrent coached football at Whisper Lake High School and raised his daughters as a single parent. Mason had seen him hiking through the woods a couple of times, two little redheaded girls bouncing along beside him.

He looked up as Mason approached and then unfolded

his lean body and got to his feet. "How you doing, Mason? Thawed out a little?"

"Barely."

"Not a good day for your boat to go down, huh?"

"It wouldn't have gone down if someone hadn't shot a hole through it."

"I heard about that. Seems like you have a bull's-eye on your back lately."

"Yeah. It does."

"You going in to visit Ms. Miller?"

"That's the plan."

"Any weapons on you?"

"No." He'd handed the soggy Ruger over to Judah and asked him to take it to a dealer who could clean and repair it.

"Heard you had a Bowie knife and a Ruger when they picked you up."

"I did."

"I guess you're like me. We like to be prepared. Chad wasn't like that. He was more a go-with-the-flow type of person."

"Chad Williams."

"I don't know any other Chad," Sam said.

"You two were good friends."

"We went to high school together, took a couple hunting trips together. We knew each other, but I can't say we were buddies."

"Was there a reason for that?"

"He was into some stuff that I'm not."

"Can you be more specific?"

"Not without getting him into trouble."

"He's already in trouble."

"You've got a point there." Sam rubbed the back of his neck and shook his head. "He liked to smoke a little weed on occasion. He partied a little too hard. He drank a little too much."

"That's not uncommon."

"It is when you're closing in on thirty. By that point, most people are getting their stuff together. Not Chad. He still heads to Portland every weekend he has off. Goes to the clubs. Picks up the women."

"Do you think that has something to do with what happened to him?"

"It's hard to say. I know he'd been acting strange the last couple of weeks. I'd even mentioned it to the sheriff."

"Strange in what way?"

"Nervous. Anxious. Twice while we were out on patrol, he pulled his gun for no reason."

"What did Judah say when you told him?"

"He talked to Chad, and I guess he asked if anything was wrong. Chad said he was fine. He tried to be calmer after that, but he was still nervous."

"Did you ask him why?" Mason queried.

"I did. He wouldn't tell me anything and I wasn't going to push. We weren't that close of friends. Of course, now I wish that we had been. Maybe I could have stopped him from whatever stupid thing he was trying to do."

"He was trying to kidnap a woman."

"Maybe."

"There's no maybe about it."

"Sure there is. We need a preponderance of evidence to convict someone, and a person isn't guilty until the conviction comes through. Besides, Chad didn't have his life together, but he wasn't violent. He didn't need to kidnap a woman to get her attention."

"He might have needed to kidnap one to get some cash."

"You've got a point. He did have $10-K in his account. Deposited it two days before he was shot."

"How do you know that?"

"We subpoenaed his bank records. We got Sally Roache's bank records today, too. Same thing. A ten-thousand-dollar deposit a week ago."

A week would have been right around the time John had died.

"I'm surprised Judah didn't tell me any of this."

"The information came in a couple of hours ago. He's been a little busy since then. He called a few minutes ago and said he was on the way, so you'll probably have a chance to discuss it with him."

"Thanks," Mason said. "I need to speak with Trinity. I'm on the list."

"Yeah. I know. Go on in. A couple of other guys are already in there."

"Thanks." Mason knocked, expecting either Cyrus or Chance to open the door.

Instead a tall, dark-haired man with dark blue eyes stood on the threshold. "Sorry. No visitors," he said and tried to close the door.

"I'm on the list."

"Mason?" Trinity called from somewhere in the room, and the guy stepped to the side, gesturing for him to enter.

"Sorry. I thought you were still hooked up to an IV under piles of warm blankets. Jackson Miller. Trinity's brother." The guy offered his hand and Mason shook it.

"Nice to meet you."

"It would be nicer if it were under better circumstances. I flew out as soon as I heard about the…" He glanced at a bed piled high with blankets. Mason assumed Trinity was in it, but he couldn't see her. "Incident," Jackson finally said.

"Is that what we're calling it?" Trinity asked. A few of

the blankets moved and Trinity peeked out. Her face was as white as the blankets, her lips tinged purple.

"Would you rather we call it 'the moment Trinity nearly died'?" Cyrus asked. He was sitting in a chair at the far side of the room, his back against the wall, his legs stretched out in front of him. Chance was a few feet away, shoulder against the wall, his eyes on Mason.

"I'd rather you all stand out in the hall and let me get dressed so we can get out of here," Trinity replied.

"You can't leave until your temperature normalizes."

"It's not going to do that while I'm lying in this breezy hospital gown," she countered.

"It will if you stay under those blankets." Mason grabbed a chair and sat next to the bed.

"You're not under any covers," she pointed out.

"I wasn't ten minutes from death, either."

She scowled. "Does everyone have to mention that?"

"Yes," her brothers and Cyrus said in unison.

She cracked a tired smile. "I know, but how about you hold off until I can find a little humor in the situation?"

"There's nothing humorous about it, sis," Jackson said. "You almost died. That's a serious thing."

"Trust me. I know it is." She shivered, pulling the blankets up to her chin, her eyes vibrant blue against her pallor. "But I've got a headache and all this talking is making it worse. Why don't you all hash out your plans in the hall? Better yet, go down to the cafeteria, get something to eat and talk about me to your heart's content. While you're doing that, I'll sleep."

"There is no way we're leaving you alone in this room," Chance began. "You'll get up, get dressed and leave, and we'll be right back where we were a few hours ago."

"I sure hope not," she said with an exaggerated shudder. "If I never see the lake or a boat again, it will be too soon."

"We're still not leaving you, and as soon as you warm up enough to get out of here, we're heading to the airport and going back to Maryland."

Trinity stiffened, but Mason didn't think her brothers noticed. They'd begun discussing the plan—how to get her out of the hospital without being noticed, how to get her to the airport in one piece. Transport from the airport to HEART headquarters in DC.

They were in the middle of the third round of *How to get her to the airport without being run off the road or intercepted before we reach the car* when Trinity touched Mason's hand, the gesture a quick brush of fingers he thought he'd imagined.

He met her eyes and she mouthed, "Save me."

So, of course, he had to.

"You look exhausted, Trinity," he said loudly, and all three men stopped talking.

"I am," she said wearily. "It's been a long couple of days and that dunk in the icy brink didn't exactly add pep to my step."

"Why don't you try to rest, then?" he continued and thought he saw a hint of a smile in her eyes.

"I would, but it's a little loud in here."

"Okay. Fine. I get it," Chance said. "We'll discuss this in the hall, but we're not going to be more than a couple of feet away, so don't try anything slick, Trinity."

"I don't have the energy for slick," she responded as her brothers left the room. Cyrus followed more slowly, his attention on Mason.

"You *are* planning to come, too, right?" he asked.

"Eventually."

"If you stay, don't be surprised if she talks you into something you have no intention of doing. She's wily."

"Thanks, Cyrus," Trinity said groggily. "I love you, too."

He smiled and walked into the hall.

Mason would have followed but Trinity grabbed his hand. "Not so fast. I need your help."

"No."

"You haven't even heard what I was going to ask."

"The answer will be no. No matter what you ask."

"Even if all I'm asking you to do is make a phone call for me?"

"To who?"

"Bryn."

"There's a phone right beside you, Trinity. How about you use that."

"You said you'd talk to her," she responded. "And, if I'm leaving in the morning, that might not happen for a while. You don't have to promise her anything. You just have to tell her that I tried."

"I'm sorry, Trinity. I'm not going to do it. I will meet with her, and I will talk to her son, but I'm not doing it over the phone, and I'm not doing it until you've prepared her for what I'm going to say." He was putting off the inevitable. He knew that, but he wasn't ready to talk to a mother facing the same kind of fear he had. He wasn't willing to look into the eyes of a kid fighting for his life.

"Why not?" Trinity demanded, her skin pale, her face gaunt. She looked like she'd been on the battlefield, her eyes haunted by things others would never understand.

He could have made an excuse, fed her a line that might have satisfied her curiosity, but he wanted her to know the truth. He wanted her to understand why he didn't work with kids. Why he never had and why he probably never would. He didn't want her to think he was callous, that he didn't care, didn't have compassion.

The fact that he cared what she thought was unsettling.

Usually he did his own thing and let other people do

theirs. He didn't judge and he didn't care if he was judged. He walked his path mostly alone and only God's opinion of that really mattered.

But now Trinity's mattered.

He didn't want her to leave town thinking the worst of him.

"I had a daughter. A lifetime ago," he said.

"I didn't—"

"Find that in your research? You wouldn't have. It's not something I talk about. She was born while I was deployed. I met her for the first time when she was six weeks old. I was a couple of months past twenty, and I'd never wanted to be a dad, but there she was, and I loved her instantly."

"Mason, you don't have to tell me this." She was still holding his hand and he could feel the fine tremors of muscles still trying to get warm.

"If I don't, you won't understand and, for some reason, I want you to."

She nodded, her expression as solemn as he'd ever seen it.

"Amelie was a sweet little girl, but she was spoiled by her grandmother and her mother and by me when I was home. Which wasn't as much as it should have been. When she was three, she got sick. My ex thought it was the flu, but Amelie never recovered. A few weeks later, they ran test to find out why she was still so sick. She had leukemia. Aggressive. Rare. Hard to treat. That's what we were told. She fought for a year, but all the fighting in the world couldn't stop the progression of the disease. We buried her a week before her birthday. It was the hardest thing I've ever done."

She didn't say a word. But she was crying, tears slipping down her cheeks and dripping onto the blankets.

"That's why I don't work with kids, Trinity. It's too hard."

"You must see your daughter in every one of them," she said.

He shook his head. "No. I see the child—whoever he or she is. I see all the things they dream of and want, and I want to fix what can't be fixed. I want to heal what only God and the doctors can. I don't like feeling helpless, and if I worked with kids, I'd feel that way every day of my life."

"I understand. I'll tell Bryn that you can't help."

"I'll her myself, and I'll talk to her son. I told you I would, and I never go back on my word."

"I haven't found your hacker yet, so you don't owe me a thing, Mason."

"You didn't, but you plan to keep looking." He was guessing.

She smiled, wiping moisture from her cheeks. "You're right. I do."

"Just be careful if you decide to look around in anyone else's systems."

"What do you mean?"

"The hacker may know he's being cyber-stalked. If so, he's probably panicked, worried that he's going to be found out before he gets the information he needs."

She frowned. "I suppose that's possible. Anyone who knows anything about computer forensics should be able to know if their system is being infiltrated. But he's got some pretty good firewalls up. It's going to take a while to get through them."

"He doesn't know that, Trinity. The guys who showed up at my place today? They took a huge chance. No one does that unless they feel desperate."

"It seems to me that they've been desperate all along."

"What they did today was risky to the point of foolishness."

"Which means I'm even closer to breaking in than I

thought I was." She sounded triumphant and excited, her hair fluttering around her cheeks as she sat up. "I need to get back in. See what it is this guy is so worried about."

"Now's not the time," he cautioned.

"There's no time like the present to do anything, Mason," she corrected, shoving aside the blankets and getting to her feet. She looked tiny, drowning in layers of hospital gowns, her feet encased in wool socks that bagged around her ankles. "My bag is in the closet. Can you grab it for me?"

He intended to say no.

He planned to tell her that she should stay in bed, get some rest, stay warm, but she smiled and he found himself grabbing the bag and handing it to her.

"Thanks. I'll be out in five," she said.

And then she walked into the bathroom and shut the door.

TWELVE

Trinity turned the lock and leaned against the door, her heart pounding wildly, her eyes still burning with tears she hadn't wanted to continue to shed. Not in front of Mason.

The story he'd shared had broken her heart.

She'd wanted to tell him that, but the words had seemed like hollow platitudes. They couldn't ease his sorrow. They couldn't bring his daughter back. All they could do was make Trinity feel like she'd tried. Since how she felt didn't matter, she'd kept her mouth shut.

She ran hot water into the sink and splashed her face with it, leaving her hands under the fiery deluge for a few seconds. Her fingers were still colorless when she pulled them out.

She'd been close to frostbite.

She'd also been close to death.

Something everyone seemed determined to remind her of. As if she needed a reminder. Her body ached, her skin burned, and her toes and fingers were on fire. She eyed her reflection in the mirror over the sink and scowled at her image.

She looked like death warmed over, her skin so pale it was nearly translucent, her hair a mess of matted tangles. Good thing she didn't care about how she looked, because she didn't think there was much she could do to improve things. Chance had grabbed the smaller of the two bags she'd had at Mason's place—the one he'd packed. There were plenty of clothes in it, but no toiletries.

She dug through the bag just to be sure and pulled out thick yoga pants and a heavy sweater, a T-shirt, jeans and about six other layers of clothes.

It took longer than she'd anticipated to dress. Her fingers were numb and clumsy, but she finally managed to tie her shoelaces, pull her hair into a ponytail and throw the hospital gowns into a laundry hamper near the door.

By the time she opened the door, she was exhausted, the need to sit almost overwhelming, but she had work to do and she didn't plan to sit around twiddling her thumbs.

Mason was still the only one in the room and he was standing at the window, staring out into the darkness. His shoulders were straight, his posture perfect, but she knew now what had caused the sorrow and loneliness in him, and she wanted to cross the room, put her hand on his arm, tell him that she understood.

She knew the emptiness that remained when someone died. She knew the hole in the heart that could never be filled. She understood all the games the mind could play and all the what-if scenarios it could create. She knew how difficult it was to move on, to live life as if the world hadn't suddenly ended.

She'd seen all those things when her sister disappeared.

She'd felt all of them.

She also knew that Mason wouldn't want her pity any more than she'd have wanted his.

"I'm ready," she said, keeping her distance because a relationship was not what she'd been looking for when she'd come to Maine. Clarity was what she'd wanted. A sense of purpose and direction and focus that would help her take the next step. Whatever that might be. She didn't need or want anything more or less than that.

Mason turned, spearing her with his dark gaze.

Her breath caught and her soul knew what her brain absolutely did not want to acknowledge—she was looking into the face of a man who was everything she should have been looking for when she'd met Dale, everything she should have wanted.

Everything she *did* want.

"You're quick, Trinity," he murmured, crossing the room and standing in front of her. "You're also as wily as Cyrus claimed."

"Not even close."

"And, yet, you're standing in the bathroom doorway, dressed and ready to leave."

"Did I talk you into doing something you didn't want to do to get here?"

"You talked me into letting *you* do what you *shouldn't* do," he responded.

"What I should or shouldn't do is a matter of opinion."

"In this case, it's a medical opinion, and you'd probably do well to listen to it."

"I plan to. The doctor told me to stay warm and hydrated. I'm wearing layers of clothes and I'm going to find something to drink. Mission accomplished." She grabbed her pack, hefted it to her shoulder and tried to move past him.

He didn't budge and the only way to the hallway was straight through him.

"Excuse me," she said, and all he did was stare her down. "It would be really nice," she continued, trying again. "If you'd move."

"How about you get back in bed and I'll bring you something to drink? What do you want?"

"To leave this room," she responded.

He smiled. "I meant to drink."

"Nothing that I can't get for myself."

"Is there some reason why you want to do that?"

"I'm planning to make a few pit stops on my way to hydrate," she admitted because she wasn't going to lie. She was going into the hall, she was going to talk her brothers into giving her a ride back to Mason's place, and then she was going to get right back to her cyber sleuthing.

"Care to elaborate?"

"I want to spend more time working on your computer. I'm getting close, or those guys wouldn't have come after us today."

"They were after you. I'm expendable."

"You're the only one who knows how to find Tate."

"Not anymore. You can hack into the system and figure out his whereabouts. Now that these guys know who you are and what you do for a living, I wouldn't be surprised if they doubled their effort to get their hands on you."

"You think that's what today was about? They know who I am?"

"I think I want to keep you safe, Trinity. That's as far as my thoughts are going right now. The best way to accomplish my goal is to have you go with your brothers. They'll take you to their safe house."

"...i.e., glorified office at HEART." She'd been in the room several times. There was a bed and a television but no phone and no computer.

"It's better than the alternative."

"Which is?"

"Death." He finally stepped aside and she was free to walk past. She didn't move. She was too busy thinking about the water lapping over the edges of Mason's boat, gurgling through the bullet hole in its side, swirling around her feet and then her ankles and then her shins.

She could have died.

She didn't want people to say it, but she couldn't make herself stop thinking about it.

"You okay?" he asked, cupping her elbow and walking her into the hallway. Her brothers were there. Just like they'd said they would be. Cyrus was there, too, talking quietly on his phone. Probably speaking to his wife. Over the past few years several members of HEART had found what Trinity could only describe as true love. She'd watched them meet, fall in love, marry. And, each time, she'd thought, *I'm next.*

Only she hadn't been.

She wouldn't be.

Which was absolutely fine. There were a lot worse things than being single.

"I'm fine," she managed to say.

He didn't respond.

She wasn't sure he would have because Chance's phone rang and he glanced at the screen.

"Odd," he said.

"What?"

"Looks like Bryn is calling me."

Odd was exactly the word Trinity would have used to describe that situation. Chance and Bryn were acquaintances. She only had his number for emergencies that involved Trinity and, as far as Trinity knew, she'd never used it.

"Has she done that before?"

"No," he said as he pressed the phone to his ear.

"Hello? Miller, here." He met Trinity's eyes, his gaze dropping to her arm and the elbow Mason was still cupping.

Mason didn't move his hand and she didn't pull away. She was too focused on Chance's conversation.

"Yes," he was saying. "She's right here. Hold on." He handed Trinity the phone.

"Hello? Bryn?" she said and, for a moment, she heard nothing. Then something that sounded like a quiet sob filled her ear.

"Bryn?" she said again, worried because her friend almost never cried.

"Yes," Bryn finally responded, her voice raspy with what could only be tears. "Thank the Lord, I finally reached you. I've been calling your cell phone for hours."

"What's wrong? Why are you crying, sweetie? Is Henry okay?" At the name, Mason's fingers tightened on her arm.

"He's gone, Trin," Bryn sobbed.

The words washed over her and she felt faint.

Henry couldn't be gone.

He was too young, too happy, too much of a fighter.

All the blood that had been in her head was pounding through her heart. She needed to sit. The only place available was the floor, so she sank, back to the wall, heart racing as she listened to her best friend cry, and imagined Henry as a baby, then a toddler, then a little boy. She'd been there through every stage. She'd laughed when he'd turned twelve and told her that he finally considered himself the man of the house. She hadn't let him hear her laughter, though, because he'd been earnest, his sincerity ringing out with every word he spoke.

Henry.

She couldn't have loved him more if he'd been her own child, and her throat felt tight with a million tears, her chest heavy with a pain that she wasn't sure she'd survive.

"What happened?" she finally managed to say. "I thought his health was stable. If I'd known it wasn't, I never would have traveled so far away." Her eyes were burning, tears sliding down her cheeks.

Someone handed her a tissue and she realized that Mason had crouched beside her and was watching her intently, his dark eyes filled with sorrow and compassion.

Her brothers were there, too. Cyrus. The deputy. All of them were watching with nearly identical looks of sorrow and pity.

"You don't understand," Bryn sobbed. "He's really gone. As in missing. He went to school this morning. He had track this afternoon. When I went to pick him up, he was gone."

"He's missing?" she repeated because she wasn't sure she'd heard right.

"Yes. I've called the police, and they're sending K-9 teams out, but… I'm scared to death, Trinity. What if they don't find him?"

"They will," she promised and then wished she hadn't.

"What will I do if they don't?"

"Don't even think about that, right now? Okay. Just concentrate on getting him home."

"I am, but I need you here. I can't do this on my own!" Bryn wailed.

"I'll be there as quickly as I can. I promise."

"I'm at the house. Come straight here when you get into town."

"I will." Trinity jumped to her feet, heading toward what she hoped was the exit. She needed to get to Maryland. She needed to be there. Now. The fact that she wasn't seemed to burn a hole in her lungs, stealing her breath, chasing every thought from her head.

Maybe the tears were doing that. They were filling her eyes so fast she could barely see.

She bumped into something, realized it was Mason,

standing in her way again. Only this time he pulled her closer, wrapped her in his arms, pressed her head to his chest. "Breathe," he said gently, and she realized that she hadn't been, that the things impeding her vision weren't just tears, they were stars, dancing around as her oxygen-starved brain struggled to keep going.

She inhaled, clutching Mason's sides as she forced herself to calm down, to think.

And the only thing she could think was that it was her fault. That somehow the men who'd been after her had gone after Henry.

"They have him," she said, moving away from the comfort of his touch and the warmth of his arms.

"Henry?"

"Yes. He's missing and they have him. I know it."

"Don't jump to conclusions, sis," Jackson said, but he was already on his phone, relaying information to someone. Probably a team member.

"It's not much of a jump," Mason said, his expression grim, his voice hard. "All they'd have had to do was ask the right questions of the right people, and they could have found out about Bryn and Henry and their relationship to Trinity."

"They wouldn't have had to ask anything," she responded woodenly, her thoughts suddenly crystal clear. "They had the album."

"What album?" Cyrus asked. He'd ended his call and was texting something.

"I put together a little photo album with pictures of Henry and Bryn. It was in my purse, so they'd have known the two were important to me." She shivered, the cold that had been with her since her dunk in the lake settling deeper.

"And you are important to them," Mason said quietly,

rubbing warmth into her cold arms. "Until they have what they want from you, they're not going to hurt Henry."

"You don't know that."

"It's as good an assumption as any," Chance cut in, his tone matter-of-fact, no hint of worry or panic.

"Chance, he's a little boy. He's going to be terrified. What if he tries to escape and they kill him? What if he doesn't and they keep him hidden away? His surgery is scheduled for next week. Without it, the cancer is going to spread and he's going to have a lower chance of survival." She could feel her anxiety building, hear the panic bubbling up in her voice.

"He's not a little boy," Chance said. "He's a smart kid with a good head on his shoulders. He won't do anything stupid and they won't, either. They want you. Not him. He's just a pawn." He tucked his phone into his pocket and turned his attention to the deputy. "We're heading to the little airport outside of Whisper Lake. Do you mind providing an escort?"

"I'll have to check with the sheriff, but—"

"By the time you do, we'll already be out the door. Since you're assigned guard duty for Trinity, it might not be a good idea to let her out of your sight," Chance said reasonably, and the deputy frowned.

"You've got a point."

"So, you'll do it?"

"I guess I will," he said. "If you guys wait in the lobby, I'll drive my cruiser up to the front door and give you rides to your vehicle."

"I'm parked in the back," Chance said.

"Me, too," Jackson added. "The easiest way to do this is to go out the back door and straight to our cars. More than likely, the perps will be watching the front doors and not paying much attention to the back. They're also looking for a patient. I'm thinking we can confuse them even more by borrowing scrubs."

"And not leaving as a group," Cyrus added.

Trinity didn't say anything, because she didn't care how they did things. She just wanted them done.

It took five minutes to come up with a plan that everyone agreed on. Sixty seconds later Mason and Trinity were in the nurses' break room, donning surgical scrubs. Mason pulled the mask down over his face, watching as Trinity did the same.

He wasn't sure how he'd gotten the assignment, but it was his job to get her to the main level and out the back door. Mostly used for delivery, it was tucked away in an alcove created by two wings of the hospital. Five flights down. Into a corridor. Turn left and keep going. Those were Chance's instructions.

"Okay," Trinity said, pulling a cap over her light brown hair. "I'm ready."

"You sure you can make it down the stairs?"

"As sure as I am that if I get my hands on the people who kidnapped Henry, I'll..." Her voice trailed off.

"What?"

"Hand them over to the authorities." Spoken aloud, the threat didn't seem nearly as intimidating as it did in her head. She walked to the door, her movements a little slower than usual, her stride a little uneven.

"Are you sure you're up to this?" he asked, glancing at his watch and then opening the door. They had six minutes to get down the stairs and out the door. Healthy, Trinity could probably have done that in half the time.

She wasn't healthy, though.

"My feet are still blocks of ice, but I can make it."

"We can grab a wheelchair and I can push you out."

"That will require taking the elevator. Which you all agreed wasn't the best idea."

True. The elevator seemed like the place most likely to be watched and Mason wanted to avoid it. But if Trinity couldn't walk down the stairs, it might be a necessity.

"We can use it if we have to."

"We don't." She stepped into the hall ahead of him and he pulled her back.

"We agreed, I was leading."

"Then go ahead and do it. My friend is in Maryland and she needs me now. Not tomorrow."

"We rush things and make mistakes," he responded, "she might not ever get the help you want to provide."

"I know," she said with a quiet sigh. "I'm sorry. I just feel like this is my fault."

"It's not."

"I had the album. I let some horrible people get their hands on it."

"And, if you could, you'd don wings and race to the rescue. Unfortunately you're no more a superhero than I am. You're going to have to take the slow road and you're going to have to be careful while you're on it."

He led the way down the hall and opened the stairwell door, scanning the corridor while Trinity walked through.

No sign of trouble. Not yet. But he was expecting it. If they'd had time, he'd have stopped at his place and grabbed a weapon. They didn't. Henry's safety was paramount and, until he was home, nothing mattered but finding him.

The trip down the stairs took less than three minutes. Once they reached the corridor, they booked it to the exit and Mason knocked on the door, listening for the signaled response. One quick rap. Three slower ones.

He opened the door, crisp, cool air sweeping in.

Cyrus was there, his attention on the back lot. He

raised a hand, signaling for Jackson and Chance to pull up. They'd decided on one vehicle. The SUV Jackson had rented. There was enough room for everyone and, according to Jackson, enough tint on the windows to prevent anyone from taking an accurate shot at the occupants.

The vehicle rolled up, lights off, engine humming quietly. They'd been idling, watching the lot, looking for signs they'd been followed. That had been as much a part of the plan as taking the stairs, riding together, having a hospital orderly take the deputy's place in front of Trinity's room.

What wasn't part of the plan was Mason boarding the plane with Trinity. It wasn't part of the group plan, anyway. It was part of his personal plan. He hadn't bothered to inform the team. He figured he'd let them know during the ride to the airport.

Cyrus opened the back door and Trinity climbed in, sliding across the bucket seat and settling into the middle, exactly the way she'd been told.

Mason climbed in after her, closing the door as Cyrus moved to the other side of the vehicle and got in.

When they pulled out of the parking lot, the deputy was behind them, driving Chance's rental rather than his marked car.

They were out of the hospital lot and on the open road within in minutes, the plan executed flawlessly. No one spoke as they wound their way along country roads and back trails. They were taking the longest, most difficult, route purposely, because it was also the least traveled.

No cars in sight.

No houses, either. Just trees. Fields. Land.

The airport was fifty miles away and, by the time they reached it, Trinity had fallen asleep, her head resting on Mason's shoulder, her body relaxed.

He didn't wake her as Jackson drove through the gates.

She needed sleep and he needed to know she was getting it. This part of the plan was the easy part. The rest? It was going to be more difficult.

"She sleeping?" Jackson asked, breaking the silence.

Mason met his gaze in the rearview mirror. "Yes."

Chance shifted in his seat, didn't seem surprised to see his sister leaning against Mason's shoulder. "The pilot is still doing safety checks, so let her sleep until we get the all-clear to board."

"How many can he take?"

"Nine. I included you in my count when I gave him the passenger list," Chance said, his tone matter-of-fact, his gaze still on his sister.

"Thanks," Mason said.

Chance finally met his eyes. "Just so you know, Gains. The jury is still out on you."

"I didn't realize a deliberation was going on."

Cyrus snorted. "We all despised her ex. We're not letting her get hurt again, so there's no way there's not going to be a deliberation."

"Trinity is old enough to know what she wants and who she wants to be with."

Jackson cut into the conversation. "And we're stubborn enough and determined enough to make sure she doesn't want to be with someone we don't approve of."

"I'm sure she appreciates your overprotective natures."

"She doesn't," Trinity mumbled, lifting her head and meeting his eyes.

She must have realized she'd been sleeping on his shoulder because she scooted away, bumping into Cyrus in her effort to put distance between them.

"I don't bite," he said, and she scowled.

"I'm not worrying about being bitten. I'm worried

about..." She shot a look in her brothers' direction and didn't continue.

"Where's the plane?" she asked instead.

"On the runway." Chance opened his door and got out. "Matt says were clear to board."

"Matt Galloway?" Trinity seemed surprised. "I thought he was flying supply planes in Africa."

"He was. We pulled him out of there last summer, remember?" Chance responded.

"I remember, but I thought he went back."

"He wanted to. His friends convinced him that it wasn't safe."

"Were you one of those friends?" Trinity asked as Chance opened Cyrus's door.

"I was the one that did most of the convincing. I don't want to see people I care about hurt, and he had a bounty on his head there."

"For what?" Mason asked, curious despite himself.

"Spreading the gospel while he delivered supplies. Faith in God drives out superstition and the local witch doctors weren't happy about that."

They moved across the airport yard, the dimly lit area providing cover Mason didn't think they'd need. Hoped they wouldn't need.

The private plane was just ahead, a long shadow in the darkness. A man moved forward to greet them as they approached. A couple of decades older than Mason, he had the stooped shoulders of someone who'd spent a lifetime lifting heavy crates.

"You made it!" Matt Galloway exclaimed, vigorously shaking Chance's hand. "We're cleared to take off in five, so let's board and get moving. Weather is perfect for a night flight. Got something for you, Trinity," he added, lifting a box from the roll-in stairs leading to the airplane door.

"What is it?"

"Don't know. The sheriff dropped it off five minutes ago. Said you'd probably need it."

She glanced in the box, a smile lightening her face as she pulled out her cell phone and keys. "The keys aren't going to do me a whole lot of good, but if I can get a charger for my phone..."

"There's one on board." Galloway gestured to the stairs. "Go ahead up. Make yourselves comfortable. The flight won't take long. A little less than two hours. You'll be back home before you even realize you were away."

Trinity laughed, but it sounded strained.

She stepped onto the stairs and headed up.

Mason followed, his shoulder still warm in the spot where her head had been resting, his thoughts racing with possibilities. He'd spent the last decade mostly alone. His choice. And he hadn't really thought about making another one, but there was something about Trinity that made him want to revisit old ideas, think through old decisions, make certain they were still apropos to his life.

He entered the small plane, ducking his head as he moved through the cabin. Trinity had chosen a seat near the back and he went there, pointing to the seat beside hers.

"This seat taken?" he asked, and she smiled, all the sweetness he'd noticed in her the first day they'd met, in her eyes.

"It will be if you take it."

"You don't want to sit next to one of your brothers?"

"I've spent a lifetime being next to them. It's good to switch up the routine," she responded, her smile broadening as he settled into the seat.

He knew he shouldn't do it, but he brushed his knuckles along her silky cheek. "You're beautiful when you smile, Trinity."

"So are you," she responded, surprising a laugh out of him.

"Thanks. I think."

"Buckle up." Galloway's voice carried through a PA system, offering advice and instruction as he started to taxi down the runway.

Mason tried to relax, but he'd never much liked flying. Not since his last stint in the military. Too many memories. Too many horrible images.

He forced himself to take a flight somewhere at least once a year. Other than that, he kept his feet firmly on the ground and his thoughts firmly in the present.

"You okay?" Trinity asked, and he nodded.

"I'm not," she responded. "I hate flying in tiny planes."

She grabbed his hand, clutching it as the plane shot into the air.

Maybe she was afraid.

But he thought she was doing it for him—offering a connection that would anchor him to the moment, keep him from slipping into the past.

"Thanks," he said, and she met his eyes.

"I really do hate flying in tiny planes," she said, her cheeks flushed with pleasure or, maybe, embarrassment.

"Thanks, anyway," he said and then leaned in and did something he hadn't even realized he'd wanted to do. Not until that moment. Not until he saw the softness in her eyes and in her face. He brushed his lips across hers, a tentative touch that left him wanting more.

She leaned in, her hand sliding up his arm and settling on his shoulder.

It felt right to be there in that moment, the past fading away as—

Something whacked him in the back and he jerked away, turning to grab a phone charger that was sliding toward the floor. Once he caught it, he looked up and realized Jackson was standing beside him.

"Watch yourself or that deliberation we're having isn't going to go well."

He returned to his seat and Mason handed the charger to Trinity, more amused than annoyed.

"My brothers are twin pains in the neck," she muttered, her flush even deeper, her hand trembling as she plugged into a power station attached to the wall.

"Your brothers care. There's nothing wrong with that."

"I guess not. Sometimes I wish they'd just be a little more subtle about it."

He laughed, and Chance shot him a hard look.

Mason returned it.

He wasn't worried about the Miller men. He was worried about Trinity, about Henry, about keeping the two of them alive. There was no room for anything else. Not yet.

Eventually though…

Eventually he thought there would be.

The tide was turning; the current that had carried him out of society was carrying him back in again. God working in His mysterious ways, bringing two people who needed each other into the right place at the right time to help each other.

All that praying he'd done, all those words he'd thrown out to God, Mason was beginning to believe they'd finally brought him to exactly the place he was supposed to be.

THIRTEEN

Trinity didn't have time to waste thinking about the kiss, but she thought about it, anyway. While the team outlined plans for finding Henry, keeping Trinity safe and putting the perpetrator behind bars, she listened. She contributed. But she also remembered…the feel of Mason's lips, the warmth of his hand, the gentleness of his touch.

By the time the plane landed, she was annoyed with herself and more than ready for some fresh air.

Of course, her brothers had different plans and she had to follow protocol, twiddling her thumbs while the men did recon, moving through the tiny Odenton Airport, searching for trouble.

She stood near the door, clutching her bag and her phone, wishing they'd hurry up.

When her phone rang, she nearly jumped out of her skin. She'd checked her messages an hour ago; listened to every heartrending voice mail Bryn had left. Then she'd tucked her phone into her pocket and tried to forget about it, because she didn't want to do what she was tempted to—listen to the messages over and over again, search for clues she wasn't going to find.

The phone rang again and her pulse jumped, adrenaline shooting through her veins.

"Calm down," she muttered as she answered it.

"Hello?"

She hadn't looked at the Caller ID, but she expected a familiar voice. Instead the tinny sound of a voice modifier filled her ears.

"Glad you finally have your phone back," the speaker said. "It's going to make things a lot easier."

"Who is this?"

"The person who's going to give you what you want. If you cooperate."

"How do you know what I want?" she hedged, moving closer to the door, praying one of the men would return.

"How about you ask the kid?"

There was a second of silence and then another voice. No modifier this time, and the voice was so familiar it made her chest ache.

"Trinity?" Henry said, his voice trembling. "Is it really you?"

"Of course it is, kiddo. Are you okay?"

"Yeah, but I want to go home."

"I'll make sure you get there."

"No. Don't," he said, the words rushing out. "I've already got cancer, so if something happens to me, it's okay. You've got years and years—"

"Henry, enough! You have years and years ahead of you, too."

"Maybe. Remember that old church where dad is buried?"

An odd question because his father was buried at Arlington.

"The brick one with the pretty steeple on it?"

"Your father isn't—"

"It's not far from home, Trinity. You can see it from the finish line."

"Enough!" someone yelled, the voice masculine and harsh.

"Henry?" she called frantically, terrified of losing her connection with him.

"Time's up," the tinny voice said, the voice modifier obviously in place again. "You talked to the kid. Now you make your choice. Get off the plane and walk to the south gate of the airport."

"How do you know—"

"I have people everywhere and I make sure to pay them well. Get off the plane, walk to the south gate."

"I don't know where that is."

"You're a very smart woman. Figure it out! You use that phone after I hang up and the boy dies. You hear me? We have it bugged. You take more than a minute to exit the plane, the same thing is going to happen."

He disconnected and she moved.

He'd given her no time to think things through. His intention, she knew, and it was effective. She shoved the phone into her pocket, keeping it on so the signal could be traced, grabbed a pen from the front of her bag and scribbled a note on the only surface available—the wall of the plane.

Henry. Brick church. Steeple. Finish line. Close to home.

That was it.

All she had time for.

She prayed it was enough.

It had to be enough because she didn't want to fail her best friend. She didn't want to fail Henry. And she didn't want to leave Mason and her brothers with more heartache and sorrow to carry home.

She walked off the plane with three seconds to spare, clambering down the stairs so quickly she almost fell.

She'd been to the airport once or twice before, and she

knew the layout vaguely, but she still had no idea where the south gate was. The moon was out, the sky clear, and she could see the path it was taking east to west. She aligned herself with that, moving south past several hangars. Beyond those, a field stretched out to what looked like road.

She headed in that direction, hoping and praying there'd be a gate somewhere at the end of her journey.

Her phone buzzed, but she ignored it, afraid to pick up, knowing there was real possibility the caller had been telling the truth. She couldn't take the chance. Not with Henry's life hanging in the balance.

She reached the edge of the field, found a tall fence topped with barbed wire. Left or right? She had to choose, and she was terrified she'd make the wrong decision.

A light flashed to her right; a quick signal that seemed to be meant for her. She followed it, walking along the fence line until she reached a gate. No one was there, but the lock had been cut with a bolt cutter and it stood open, the road beyond it empty.

Go back, her mind whispered, but she didn't dare listen.

Henry needed her, and she wasn't going to save herself and sacrifice him. She stepped onto the road, saw another flash of light. It was leading her somewhere and she had no choice but to go. She walked quickly, her heart pounding frantically, her phone buzzing over and over again. The team was trying to find her. How long would it take for the police to find her signal and follow it?

She stepped between shrubs that crowded into the road, was pushing through thick foliage, when she felt movement behind her.

She had a split second to react, to turn toward the sound, to raise her arm to block whatever was swinging toward her head. It slammed into her arm and the bone snapped. She felt that, then felt a glancing blow to her cheek as it grazed the side of her face. She fell, the pain from her arm excruciating, her need to cry out, to moan, to pull the arm in close, overridden by her need to survive.

She closed her eyes, faked unconsciousness.

Someone kicked her in the ribs and she forced herself not to flinch.

"She's out," a man said.

"Then stop standing around like an idiot and pick her up. Her buddies probably aren't too far behind," a woman responded.

That surprised Trinity and she was tempted to open her eyes to take a peek. She was afraid to risk it, so she stayed limp as she was lifted from the ground, carried for a count of twenty, and dumped into the back of either a truck or a van.

A door closed and she waited, listening to the voices of her captors as they moved around the vehicle and got into the front.

"That worked out better than I'd hoped," the woman said. "The General will be pleased."

"I hope you're not planning to tell him. He told you to leave well enough alone."

"You know what the punishment for treason is, Mack? Death," she snarled.

"Your husband knew that when he—"

"Shut up! If she wakes up, I don't want her to hear anything."

"Wakes up? You'll be fortunate if she's still alive when we get to the—"

"I said be quiet!" the woman shrieked.

"You know what, Doris? I didn't sign up for crazy. So how about you transport the woman back, talk her into getting you into Gains's computer system, and do everything else I've been doing for the past month."

"You've been paid well."

"Compared to what your husband raked in, I was paid squat." He opened a door and Trinity could feel cold wafting in. Her arm hurt so badly she could barely move. Which was probably for the best. Doris sounded like a nutcase. The guy she was with was a mercenary, and, between the two of them, she didn't think she stood a chance of surviving.

That being the case, she needed to take a few chances. Because if her chances of survival were nothing, she couldn't hurt them by trying to escape.

She opened her eyes just enough to see the tan interior of the vehicle. A van of some sort. Probably a minivan because it had a hatchback. She was alone in the back. She was sure of that, and she opened her eye completely, the interior lights giving her a clear view of the stained carpet and the scuffed walls. The rear window was tinted, so there was no way anyone would see her lying there. She could open the hatch once the engine started. Jackson had made her practice that trick dozens of times when she was a kid.

Just in case, he'd always said, and she'd laughed because "just in case" was never going to happen. Only, it was happening and she was going to have to remember that long-ago skill, because when they reached their destination, she was dialing 9-1-1 and then launching an attack.

A one-armed attack, but it was better than allowing Henry to be hurt. And that was what would happen. They might use him as a pawn for a while, but eventually they'd have what they wanted and he'd be nothing but a liability.

"Hold on, Mack," the woman said. "We part ways after this is over. That was the agreement."

"We made the agreement before I knew you were nuts."

"If I'm crazy it's because I'm worried about the General."

"Worried about his money is more like it. At least I

went into this with the right motivation. I wanted to help my old mentor," Mack said.

"Give me a break. You went into this for the money—and you'll get the money. But first we have to find Tate. That's the goal. That's the mission."

"That's the final destination," he muttered as if he'd heard it all a dozen times before, but he closed the door. The interior lights went off and Trinity was enveloped in darkness.

She knew where the hatch was. She knew what she needed to do, but the pain in her arm was stealing her energy. She needed to focus, stick with the plan, figure out a secondary one in case the first didn't work.

Church. Steeple. Finish line. Home.

Henry had been giving her a message. He was smart, and he'd probably been thinking it through since he'd been kidnapped. But, for the life of her, she couldn't remember a church with a steeple near her house or his.

"The final destination," the woman said, "is somewhere far away from this country and all her needy, grasping people."

"Not very nice thoughts for someone who once served."

"I served because I needed money. I didn't sit on my butt and collect—"

"How about we skip this part and get out of here?" Mack asked. The engine sputtered and then roared.

Trinity braced herself, afraid her arm would be jostled by bumps in the road and she'd scream in agony.

Think! Focus!

She used the noise of the engine to mask the sound of her good hand skimming across scratchy carpet, finding the latch that held the hatch closed.

Something thumped against the side of the van and she froze.

"What was that?" Mack asked.

"I don't—"

Glass shattered and the woman screamed. Trinity didn't wait to be told what was going on. She pulled the latch, jumped out of the vehicle, stumbling as her feet hit the ground. The van was rolling away, thumping as flat tire met blacktop, and she was running in the opposite direction, Henry's words chanting through her mind…

Church. Steeple. Finish line. Home.

And suddenly she knew.

She could remember it clearly. Henry's first track meet, sitting in the stands with Bryn, cheering him on. Congratulating him on his first-place finish after he'd crossed the finish line. He'd pointed to a church across the street from the track and told her that God had given wings to his feet.

He'd only been seven and Trinity had thought him wise beyond his years. She'd forgotten that. Just like she'd forgotten the church with is brick facade and beautiful steeple.

She slammed into something, her injured arm smashing against it. She gagged, the pain so intense she was on her knees vomiting into her the dirt.

"We need an ambulance," someone said and she realized Mason was beside her, a pistol in his hand.

"No ambulance," she muttered.

"Your arm," he began, and she could see what he did—her forearm bent at an unnatural angle.

"I know where Henry is. He's probably not alone."

"Trinity, your arm is broken badly."

"My heart will be broken worse if something happens to Henry," she responded.

His jaw tightened, his eyes flashed, and then he was moving, using his jacket as a sling, tying it around her neck and easing her arm in it.

She almost passed out.

Almost.

But she knew if she did, the ambulance would come and take her away and everything she knew about Henry would be lost until she regained consciousness again.

"How is she?" Chance called, jogging toward them, a streak of blood on his cheek.

"I'm fine," she lied.

"She knows where Henry is," Mason told him. "She wants to go there."

"Tell us where, Trinity. We'll bring him home," Chance said gently, stepping between her and the van. She could still see. Cyrus and Jackson were there with two other men. One of them frisking a skinny woman with white hair. The other frisking a tall, lanky man.

"It will be easier to show you, and faster." She started walking, not really sure where she was headed. Maybe to find a ride.

"You need to sit." Mason touched her shoulder and tried to steer her toward a patch of grass that he probably wanted her to sit in.

"I need to go to the church."

"You're not making any sense, Trinity," her brother said, and she swung around to face him, all her fear and frustration bubbling out.

"I promised Bryn that Henry would come home. I'm going to make sure that promise is fulfilled. I don't care how long it takes, and I don't care what I have to do. I'm going to find him. I'm going to make sure he's delivered back to his mother. After that, I'll go to the hospital and have my arm set, but not before. Does that make sense?" she demanded, and he cocked his head to the side, eyed her steadily for a few heartbeats.

"You've made yourself abundantly clear, Trinity."

"And?"

"You'd better do exactly what I tell you. Every single thing. No matter how much you might not want to. Understood."

"You've made yourself abundantly clear," she replied.

Chance didn't even crack a smile.

"I'm getting a car. Give me five minutes, and then we'll head out."

She waited until he was several feet away and then she puked again, kneeling by the edge of the road, heaving until she could barely breathe, her arm throbbing steadily, her cheek throbbing, too.

When she finally straightened, Mason was there, handing her a piece of gum and a cloth she thought might have been part of his shirt. "Better?" he asked.

"No." But she popped the gum into her mouth, wiped the cloth across her face and told herself she was going to be okay.

Then she took the hand he offered and let him lead her across the road and away from the van. Up a small hill and into a parking lot. Headlights flashed and he slid his arm around her waist, offering extra support as they moved in that direction. "That's your brother."

"How do you know?"

"We were on our way here when I decided to go back and check on you."

"I was doing fine."

"I think we can both agree that you weren't. If I'd been a minute later, I wouldn't have seen you exit the cabin, and you'd be halfway down the road heading for—"

"A church," she said. "Near Henry's old elementary school."

"You think they have him there?"

"I don't know, but he tried to send me a message while we were talking, and the only thing I got from it was that."

"Then we'll check it out, but if he's not there, you're going to the hospital."

"I promised Bryn that Henry would be okay."

"Do you think that promise is going to matter if you and Henry are both dead?" he asked, the harsh question making her wince.

"Bryn—"

"This isn't just about Bryn. This about your parents. Your brothers. Your friends." He took a breath. "It's about me. I care about you. I want to see what my future will be with you in it, and I'm not willing to see you hurt because of your determination to prove your worth to people who already know your value."

He was right.

She knew he was.

She'd spent years trying to prove her value to people who already understood it. A waste of time and a waste of energy, and here she was, trying to do it again, because, maybe, she really needed to prove something to herself.

She wanted to tell Mason that.

She wanted to say that she cared, too. Wanted to say that a future together would be a whole lot better than a future alone.

Dozens of words were there.

Dozens of things she could have said that would have let him know how deeply she'd begun to care for him.

Her heart thumped with the weight of them, her arm throbbing in time with it, and the words stuck in her throat, because she was terrified that she'd say too much or not enough and ruin whatever it was they were building together.

They'd reached Chance's sedan and he'd opened the door, was gesturing for her to climb in.

Mason walked to the other side of the car and her opportunity was lost to bad timing and bad experience and her own annoying cowardice.

A brick church.

A steeple.

A finish line.

And home.

They'd found a place that ticked every one of those boxes—a pretty little church on a pretty little yard that faced Henry's elementary school.

Mason could see the track from his position at the corner of the street. He could see the sign posted in the front of the church building. It was being renovated, an addition onto the back, the congregation sharing a sister church until the building was ready.

"What do you think?" Chance asked, his attention focused on the front door.

He might have been talking to Mason, but it was more likely he was speaking the chief of police. He'd arrived before they had, responding to a call Chance had made.

"I think we wait for the K-9 team. They've been tracking the boy. We'll see if they catch a whiff of him around the building and then we'll—"

A light appeared in one of the church windows, there and gone so quickly they would have missed it if they hadn't been watching.

"Henry..." Trinity murmured, taking a step toward the building.

"Don't jump the gun, Trinity," Mason said, taking her good arm and holding her back. The other arm was in his improvised sling, but he knew it was swelling and that the pain was excruciating.

"He's in there. I know he is."

"And the people he's with are probably armed and dangerous," he noted.

"And they're going to panic when that woman—"

"Doris Samson," the chief confirmed. "She's wife to General William Samson. He's—"

"Facing court-martial proceedings." Mason cut into the chief's explanation.

"Right. The guy she was with was in one of Samson's barracks. They worked together for a number of years and Mack was probably very aware of what Samson was doing."

"They all wanted the money," Trinity said. "That was the motivation. If Henry dies because—"

"He's not going to die," Mason responded, letting his hand slide from her arm to her nape. Her skin felt clammy and cool.

"I hope you're right, Mason," she responded, still watching the church as if Henry would somehow appear in front of it.

The light flashed again. This time in another window.

"A signal maybe?" Chance suggested.

"Probably looking for the boss to return," the chief responded. "I have two men on the ground near the back of the property. I'm sending them in."

"I thought you wanted to wait until the K-9 teams arrived."

"I planned to, but if the guy inside is getting antsy, the kid might be in imminent danger."

"Do you really think—" Mason began. He didn't have time to finish. Glass broke and someone screamed, the sound filled with terror and panic.

"Henry!" Trinity yelled, and, as if her words had conjured him, the front door opened and a boy ran out. Long and lanky, limping a little as he sprinted away from the church, a taller, heavier person behind him. Not a police officer. The guy looked like a thug, the streetlights glinting off a gun pointed straight at the kid's head.

"No!" Trinity shouted, and it was enough to stop both for a split second. The man glanced in their direction, the gun swinging toward them.

"Police! Drop it!" the police chief yelled.

A shot rang out and the man fell, the gun tumbling from his hand.

"Trinity!" Henry pivoted and headed in their direction, running with that swift, limping gait.

"Trinity!" he called again, and she darted forward just as the guy on the ground rolled over, snatched up his gun again.

Mason leaped forward, knocking Trinity to the ground, her scream choked off as she landed on her broken arm.

And then there was just Henry, running toward him, the gunman aiming for his back.

Mason was up and moving, Chance in his periphery, gun drawn, stance wide.

Chance fired as Mason dove for the kid, dragged him to the ground, a bullet slamming into the pavement near his head, bits of cement and dirt flying into his face as another shot rang out and another.

Then there was silence, complete except for the frantic breathing of the kid he was shielding.

He looked around. Saw the gunman spread-eagled on the ground, an officer frisking him. Chance near his sister, feeling for a pulse and shouting into his phone.

Mason stood, dragging Henry with him.

"Trinity!" the kid said, breaking away and running to her side.

Mason followed, crouching next to her, searching for signs that she'd been shot. There was no blood. No bullet wounds. Just a bruise on her cheek and the arm he didn't dare touch.

"You called for an ambulance?" he asked, and Chance nodded grimly.

"It's on the way."

"And I'm not going in it," Trinity muttered without opening her eyes. "Not until we have Henry."

"You do have me," Henry said, touching her cheek.

She opened her eyes, smiling as she looked into Henry's face. Her gaze shifted from the boy to Chance and then to Mason.

Something changed when she looked at him. The smile softened, her tension eased, and she held out her good hand.

"I thought you said you weren't a superhero," she said as he took it.

"Did I?"

"Yes. Remember? My bat cave comment? You said you'd have one if you were a superhero."

"I'm not."

"No? I'm pretty sure you were flying when you tackled me from behind," she said.

He smiled, pressing a kiss to her knuckles and then to her cheek.

"Maybe for you, I managed to achieve the impossible," he said, and she smiled.

"Gross," Henry said.

Chance laughed. "You won't think so when you're our age, kid."

"You especially won't think it when you meet the right woman," Mason added.

"Is that what I am?" Trinity asked.

"If you want to be," he responded.

She sighed. "Mason, I walked into your life and brought nothing but chaos with me."

"I've decided I like chaos."

"Do you also like dragging me from a lake, saving me from drowning, rescuing me from kidnappers, and—"

"Yes." He cut her off as an ambulance crew arrived and lifted her onto a gurney.

"Are you sure?" she asked. "Because I'm not sure you know what you're getting yourself into."

"I know exactly what I'm getting into," he responded.

"Yeah?"

"Yeah."

"Now, how about you stop talking and let the ambulance transport you? Henry and I are coming along, too," he said, touching the boy's shoulder.

"I'd rather go home," Henry said. "I need to see my mom. I need to tell her that I'm okay."

"Your mom will meet you at the hospital, son," Chance said.

"And the ride in the ambulance will give us a chance to get to know each other," Mason added.

"Why would we want to do that?" Henry asked, crossing his scrawny arms over his chest.

"Because after your surgery and your recovery, you and I are going to meet and I'm going to make you a prosthetic leg that you'll be wearing at the Paralympics one day."

"You're Mason Gains?" Henry asked, his eyes widening.

"I am."

"My mom was telling me about you. Wait until she hears that this!"

"She'll hear it sooner if you get in the ambulance," Trinity said.

Henry nodded, allowing himself to be lead away by an EMT.

The rest of the ambulance crew followed, carrying the gurney, Trinity lying pale and silent as they moved her.

Mason ignored the attendant's comment that there wasn't room, climbing aboard the ambulance, taking a seat beside Henry and smiling as the kid chatted with Trinity. They could have been mother and son, and he could finally see the bond that had sent her to a stranger's doorstep.

He'd be forever grateful for that.

Trinity glanced his way, grabbed his hand and pulled him down so she could speak without shouting.

"Thank you," she said.

"Once I saw him, I couldn't say no."

"You could have. We both know it."

"Maybe I should have said that once I saw you, I couldn't say no," he replied, kissing her temple, his lips linger for a moment longer than necessary.

"Like I said..." Henry muttered. "Gross."

Trinity laughed then groaned, closing her eyes as the ambulance bounced over ruts in the road.

"You okay?"

"I will be," she murmured, her eyes still closed, her hand still in his. She didn't release her hold. Not as they reached the hospital. Not she was unloaded. Not even when they wheeled her into the building, Henry in a wheelchair beside her.

They reached the emergency ward and a nurse touched her shoulder. "Ma'am, this is where you and your husband are going to have to say goodbye."

Mason could have corrected her. Trinity could have, too.

Neither did.

Instead, Trinity squeezed his hand and released it. "See you when I'm on the mend?"

"If I have my way," he replied, "you'll be seeing me every day for the rest of your life."

She smiled. "I'm counting on it."

She turned her attention to Henry, gave him an encouraging nod. "Ready, kiddo? Let's get this done."

And then she offered Mason a quick wave, closed her eyes and was wheeled away.

FOURTEEN

Winter came quickly in Maine.

That's what Trinity was thinking as she turned her Jeep onto the access road that led to Mason's property. The fall colors had faded to browns and grays, the ground was sprinkled with a light powdering of snow, and everywhere she looked, winter seemed to be. Even the lake was still and calm, the surface icy near the shore.

"Wow!" Henry said from his seat in the back.

She glanced in the rearview mirror, smiling as she saw the excitement on his pale face. He'd weathered the surgery, was recovering well from the amputation, and he was ready for the first step in the process of creating a prosthetic leg.

"Are you sure Mason really wants to do this?" Bryn whispered. "I'd hate to have gotten Henry's—"

"I can hear you, Mom."

"It's not a secret, sweetie. You've been through a lot, and I don't want you to suffer more."

"Suffering is sitting in the house being bored out of my mind. This—" he waved out the window "—is an adventure of the first order. Even if Mason sends me away, it will be worth it."

"He won't," Trinity assured them both, releasing her

grip on the steering wheel and shaking out her left hand. She still had problems with the arm, the surgery to reset the bones causing minor nerve damage. Or, maybe, the break had done that.

It didn't matter.

The results were the same.

Her speedy typing days were at an end, but she'd still managed to track the person who'd hacked into Mason's computer system. Spending three days in the hospital with nothing to do but stare at the walls and wait for Mason to visit had given her plenty of time to go back through the trails she'd been following.

This time, she hadn't been booted back because the hacker had already been tossed in jail. Mack Danner had as much computer expertise as Trinity. It was a shame he'd used it for criminal activity.

Of course, Doris Samson had tried to throw him under the bus, claiming the scheme to get rid of the sole witness to her husband's crime had been Mack's idea. Trinity thought Doris was a lot more deeply involved, but that wasn't for her to decide. The authorities had things under control, and she was leaving the investigating to them.

After Mack's arrest, Tate had agreed to reenter witness protection. With the trial looming, the military police and federal government had put extra man power into keeping him safe. So far, the effort seemed to be paying off.

That was great news for him.

The news for Sally Roache hadn't been nearly as wonderful. She'd been arrested on charges of conspiracy to commit murder. She'd agreed to a plea deal in exchange for testifying against Mack. According to her, Mack had approached John and offered him an opportunity to ruin Mason's life the way that his had been ruined. Allowing confidential client information to be leaked was a sure-fire way to destroy the business Mason had worked so hard to build.

At least, that's what Mack had claimed when he'd offered John twenty-thousand dollars to gain access to Mason's secure server and find out where Tate Whitman was hiding.

An easy job.

That's what Mack had said.

John had taken the first half of the payment, deposited it in their account, and then had second thoughts. He'd wanted to back out of the deal, and she thought he would have if he hadn't died.

His death seemed convenient, and the DA was pouring over John's autopsy report, hoping to find evidence that it had really been a murder.

Once John had died, Sally had believed her dealings with Mack were over. But, he called her the day after John's death and threatened to kill her if she didn't find a way to get Mason away from his Maine home.

She'd complied.

Not for money, but out of fear.

That was the story she told to everyone who would listen.

A jury would decide whether or not she was telling the truth.

Trinity would testify at Mack's trial, but she wouldn't spend her time thinking about it or worrying about it. God was in control and His plans for her life were so much better than hers could ever be.

She smiled as she pulled up in front of Mason's house.

This was better than anything she ever could have dreamed or planned or even asked for. Mason was the kind of guy who kept his promises, who built her up, who listened and cared and made her feel like the only person who really mattered to him.

As a bonus, her parents loved him.

Her brothers liked him.

Every team member who'd showed up on Mason's doorstep claiming to have questions about the pending criminal case against Doris came back to Maryland with good reports.

And, Trinity?

She was in love.

She could admit that to herself even if she hadn't said it to anyone else. Mason was everything she hadn't known she needed, everything she'd had no idea was missing from her life.

The front door opened as she got out of the car, and he was there, wearing old flannel and faded jeans and a smile that made her heart sing.

She ran toward him, throwing herself into arms she knew would always be there.

"Finally," he murmured against her hair. "I thought you'd never get here."

"It's a long drive."

"And it's been forever since I've seen you." He kissed her once. Twice. The third time, he lingered, pulling her close, stealing her breath.

"Gross," Henry said, moving toward them on crutches, his face wreathed in a happy smile.

"You look good, kid," Mason said. "How's the leg?"

"I don't know. We're not on speaking terms," he said, and Mason laughed.

"Hold on to that sense of humor. It'll be a great asset in the future." He turned his attention to Bryn, his hands still on Trinity's waist, his hold light and steady and just exactly right. "How are you doing, Bryn?"

"Fantastic. I thought this day would never come and, now that it's here, I'm feeling pretty proud of myself for keeping my mouth closed," she responded, smiling at Mason and then at Trinity. "It's finally your turn, hun. And, it's about time," she said quietly.

"My time for what?"

The front door opened again, and her parents walked out, arm in arm, just like they always were. Jackson was behind them, his daughter in his arms, his family crowded close. Chance shoved through the crowd, walking out onto the stoop with Stella on one arm and Gertrude on the other.

And, Trinity knew.

Before Mason said a word, before the entire group moved toward her, surrounded her, pulled out cameras and phones and packets of tissue.

She knew, and she looked into Mason's eyes, into his familiar and wonderful face, and she saw everything she hadn't known she should want, everything she hadn't dared ask God to give her. And she wanted to hold on to it forever, to cherish it the way it should be, because what she had with Mason was the best and finest gift she had ever been given.

"I love you, and I will," she proclaimed before he asked her to marry him, all the feelings gushing out in those two phrases.

He laughed, pulling a box from his coat pocket, kissing her before he opened it.

"I love you, too," he murmured against her lips. "Forever and a day. Probably longer."

"Forever is always longer," she replied, her hands on his shoulders, the soft old flannel and the warmth of his skin beneath making her long to pull him closer.

"Nothing will ever be long enough. Not when it comes to spending my life with you. Will you marry me?"

"Like I said—I love you. And I will. Forever and a day. Probably longer."

Her family cheered, Bryn cried and Henry stood a few steps away, looking straight into her eyes and mouthing, "Maybe it isn't so gross, after all."

She laughed, offering her hand as Mason took the ring from the box and slid the beautiful, ruby solitaire on her finger.

"You didn't seem like a diamond kind of woman," he said, and she smiled, throwing her arms around him, pulling him close.

"How do you do that, Mason?" she asked.

"Read you so well?"

"Make me so happy," she responded, and the whole world faded as he cupped her face, looked into her eyes and kissed her again.

* * * * *

Dear Reader,

When I have goal, I go after it with dogged determination. This is great when my plan and God's are in alignment. It's tougher when what I'm striving for isn't God's best for me. In *Mistaken Identity*, Trinity Miller realizes that something she's spent years working toward isn't going to happen. She can't understand why her dream isn't part of God's plan, and she can't imagine anything better than what she had in mind.

Then she meets Mason Gains.

At first, he's just a recluse who may be able to help her friend. But when a quick weekend trip becomes a life-and-death struggle, Trinity learns that God's plan is much more wonderful than hers could ever be.

I hope you enjoy the seventh book in the Mission: Rescue series, and I pray that whatever path you walk, God's love and faithfulness will guide you.

Blessings,

Shirlee McCoy

COMING NEXT MONTH FROM

Love Inspired® Suspense

Available April 4, 2017

GUARDIAN

Classified K-9 Unit • by Terri Reed

When widow Alicia Duncan witnesses a crime, the perpetrator is dead set on silencing her for good. And it's up to FBI K-9 agent Leo Gallagher and his trusty chocolate-Labrador partner to keep her and her young son safe.

DANGEROUS TESTIMONY

Pacific Coast Private Eyes • by Dana Mentink

After private investigator Candace Gallagher agrees to testify against a shooter, the single mother finds herself—and her daughter—targets of a gang leader. But her family friend, former navy SEAL Marco Quidel, is determined to protect them both...and help bring the criminals to justice.

FALSE SECURITY

Wilderness, Inc. • by Elizabeth Goddard

As Olivia Kendrick tracks her missing brother through the Oregon wilderness with her ex-boyfriend, former detective Zachary Long, someone will stop at nothing—even murder—to make sure they never find him.

RANCH HIDEOUT

Smoky Mountain Secrets • by Sandra Robbins

Undercover FBI agent Gabriel Decker has a mission: make sure Elizabeth Madison Kennedy lives to testify about the mafia hit she witnessed. A Smoky Mountain ranch seems like the perfect place to hide...until the location is leaked and thugs intent on killing her arrive.

PLAIN TARGET

Amish Country Justice • by Dana R. Lynn

Jess McGrath will prove her brother was murdered...even if her investigation puts her own life in danger. But with a killer's target on her back and her high school nemesis, paramedic Seth Travis, as her only ally, she must disappear into Amish country until she finds the truth.

FINAL VERDICT • by Jessica R. Patch

Defense attorney Aurora Daniels's current case isn't the first where someone threatens her. But when attempts are actually made on her life, she knows this time is different. And while they constantly clash over matters of the law, Sheriff Beckett Marsh is the only person she can trust to save her.

When one of their own goes missing, an elite FBI K-9 unit will stop at nothing to bring him back.

Read on for a sneak preview of
GUARDIAN,
the first book in the exciting new series
Classified K-9 Unit.

The daylight broke over the horizon of the industrial district, and muted morning light slashed through the high windows of the large two-floor warehouse. FBI agent Leo Gallagher pressed his back to the wall inside the cavernous structure's entrance. The air was cool but heavy with a mix of anticipation and caution.

His heart rate increased. Not much, but enough that he took a calming breath. He tightened his hold on the leash of his canine partner, a chocolate Labrador named True.

The open floor plan of the bottom level was filled with containers and pallets that provided too many hiding places. That could be a problem. Shadows lurked above and in the recesses of the corners.

Almost time? Leo glanced at fellow FBI agent Jake Morrow and his canine, a Belgian Malinois named Buddy.

Behind his tactical face guard, Jake nodded and signaled for Leo and True to proceed into the murky depths of the purported hideout of the notorious Dupree syndicate. The criminal organization that the elite FBI K-9 unit had been working around the clock to bring down for months.

LISEXP0317

But every time the team got close, the crime boss, Reginald Dupree, and his second in command, his uncle Angus Dupree, managed to escape.

Not going to happen this time. The first time could have been coincidence, but after the second and third times, something else was going on. That was why Leo's boss had been tight-lipped about this raid. No one outside the tight circle of the team knew of today's operation in case there was a leak.

True's ears perked up. The scruff of his neck rose. He emitted a deep growl from his throat.

Breath stalling, Leo paused, scanning the area for whatever threat his partner sensed.

Four men with automatic weapons appeared from around the sides of the two containers. A barrage of gunfire erupted. The deafening noise bounced off the walls.

Leo's heart revved into overdrive. His pulse pounded in his ears as he dropped to one knee to return fire.

"Down!" Leo shouted to True.

LISEXP0317